Vicki Blum

The Promise
of the
Unicorn

Cover by
Albert Slark

Illustrated by
David Bordeleau

Vicki Blum

The Promise
of the
Unicorn

Cover by Albert Slark
Illustrated by David Bordeleau

Scholastic Canada Ltd.

Toronto New York London Auckland Sydney
Mexico City New Delhi Hong Kong Buenos Aires

Scholastic Canada Ltd.
175 Hillmount Road, Markham, Ontario L6C 1Z7, Canada

Scholastic Inc.
555 Broadway, New York, NY 10012, USA

Scholastic Australia Pty Limited
PO Box 579, Gosford, NSW 2250, Australia

Scholastic New Zealand Limited
Private Bag 94407, Greenmount, Auckland, New Zealand

Scholastic Ltd.
Villiers House, Clarendon Avenue, Leamington Spa,
Warwickshire CV32 5PR, UK

Map by Paul Heersink/Paperglyphs

Edited by Laura Peetoom

National Library of Canada Cataloguing in Publication

Blum, Vicki, 1955-
The promise of the unicorn / by Vicki Blum;
illustrated by David Bordeleau.

ISBN 0-439-98967-1

I. Bordeleau, David II. Title.

PS8553.L86P76 2002   jC813'.54   C2002-901255-4

5 4 3 2 1   Printed and bound in Canada   02 03 04 05

To the students and staff of
St. Mary's School

"And it shall be a habitation of dragons . . . "
Isaiah 34:13

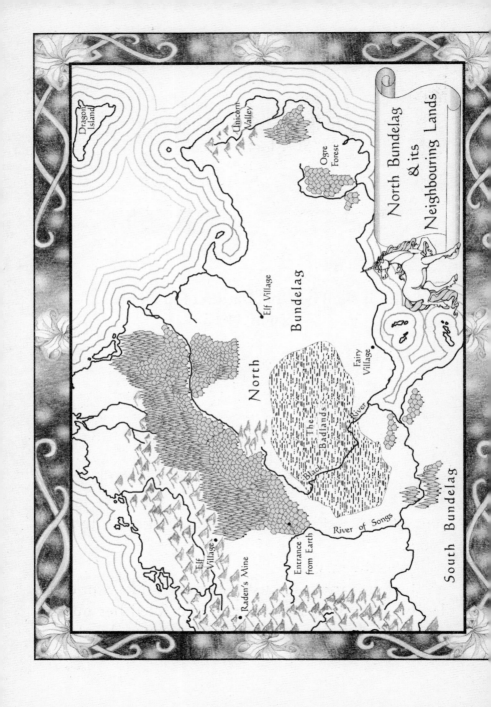

North Bundelag
& its
Neighbouring Lands

Dragon Island

Unicorn Valley

Ogre Forest

Elf Village

North

Bundelag

The Black Badlands

Fairy Village

River

River of Songs

Elf Village

Raden's Mine

Entrance from Earth

South Bundelag

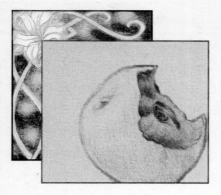

Chapter 1

Arica knew something was wrong the moment she opened the door.

It wasn't because the door was slightly ajar and swung open beneath her touch, even though her mother didn't usually leave the house unlocked. It wasn't the half-dried trail of mud all down the front hallway, either. And it wasn't even the quiet murmur of voices drifting out to her from the living room.

It was the magic.

She felt it the instant she stepped inside. It prickled over her skin like icy rain and filled her mind with a murky, nameless foreboding. She took a deep breath to steady herself and pulled the door closed behind her while the dread she was feeling tightened in her stomach like knots of pain.

There was no place this magic could have come from except North Bundelag.

She had gone there on three different occasions by falling through the crack in her grandmother's kitchen floor, and had spent a lot of time getting to know the marvellous creatures of that land. By now she was quite familiar with the feel and flavour of everything found there, including this.

She was certain that it wasn't anything good.

There were many different kinds of magic found in Bundelag. There was the magic of the unicorns, a kind that was blue-bright and warm and raced like tiny bubbles through her veins. Then there was her grandmother the Fairy Queen's kind of magic. It was calm and full of wisdom, like Grandmother, and had a certain no-nonsense quality to it. The elves' magic was fresh and solid, the magic of the earth and of growing things. Once she had encountered the magic of the ogres and it was a good kind too, though quite strange and unpredictable.

Shadow, the rebel unicorn, also had a peculiar magic. She had come up against it several times in the past and wasn't eager to repeat the experience any time soon. His magic was thick and dark and filled with a kind of bitter poison, just as he was.

Then there was the magic that her uncle Raden possessed. It was dark, like Shadow's, but instead of being fuelled by pain and anger, it was fuelled by selfishness and greed. Its aim was always to conquer and destroy. It was the most powerful magic she had found in Bundelag — and the most evil.

It was her uncle Raden's magic that Arica was feeling now.

She tiptoed down the hallway, hardly daring to breathe. Pausing beside the doorway to the living room, she listened for voices or the sound of movement — anything that might give her a clue as to what was going on. The murmuring had ceased. She waited in the silence, and while her stomach played leapfrog beneath her ribs she wondered if her uncle was here, now, and what terrible thing was about to happen because of his presence — or had already happened. She swallowed the thick lump that rose in her throat, clenched her teeth, and stepped into the living room.

What she saw was every bit as dreadful as she had feared.

Her mother sat cross-legged on the sofa smiling at a man who was seated in the easy chair across from her. Her father's chair, thought Arica. Her uncle had no right to be there. Arica's next thought was to wonder how he'd managed to make his way undetected from South Bundelag, where he'd been exiled, across the border into North Bundelag and then all the way to Bundelag's last entrance to this world.

Then the man in the chair looked up, and his eyes met Arica's. And there was no more room for thought, only for trying to control the wild trembling that rose up inside of her.

This was the man who only a few weeks ago had locked Arica and her cousin Connor inside a dark, damp dungeon while he schemed to get to the *Book of Fairies* before they did. This was the man who had turned the Shadow unicorn's angry magic against all of his kind, nearly bringing an end to the unicorns of Bundelag. This was the man who had made slaves of elves and unicorns while he schemed with the trolls to betray his homeland to the greedy South. This man was her most bitter enemy — and he was relaxing in her very own living room in her father's favourite chair, as if he had just dropped in for a friendly family visit.

"Hello, my dear," he said in that mocking tone she knew so well. "It's nice to see you again."

"What do you want?" Arica asked coldly. She wasn't going to waste time by playing Raden's polite little game. If there was one thing she had learned about him, it was that her uncle never did anything without a reason. And his reasons were always good for him and not so good for anyone who happened to get in his way.

"Arica," her mother protested, "where are your manners?"

Cold fingers tickled their way down Arica's spine. Not because of what her mother had said — Arica was used to her mother correcting everything Arica did, from the way she held her fork to the tone in her voice when she said please and thank you. But never before had Arica heard her mother's voice sound so sweet, so mild. So unaware of the danger that sat across from her.

"Mother!" Arica cried, trying to drag her mother's enraptured stare away from Raden's face.

Her mother's gaze turned toward her, clearly with some reluctance. Her eyes had a vague, unfocussed look and her lips smiled foolishly at nothing.

"Let her go," Arica said, her voice rising in alarm. "It's me you want, not her."

Raden raised one black eyebrow in mock surprise. "On the contrary," he replied, "*she's* the one I came for."

Something lurched sickly inside of Arica. She leaned against the arm of the sofa for support as her knees went weak beneath her. "What do you want with her?" she managed to gasp out as she choked down a growing feeling of panic. "She hasn't done you any harm, and she knows nothing. Leave her out of this."

"Have some fruit, dear," said Mother, pushing a

bowl of fresh peaches across the coffee table with one of her hands. "It's a gift from your uncle. Did you know your father had a brother? I didn't — your father has always been so mysterious about his past. But here's his brother, come from far away, and see the nice peaches he brought us."

Arica stared at her babbling mother, then at the peaches. Poisoned fruit only happened in fairy tales. But her uncle *was* a fairy, and what better way was there to poison someone? She yanked the bowl away from her mother. That's when she saw the half-eaten peach resting in her mother's other hand.

Arica dropped the bowl and whirled toward Raden. "What have you done to her?" she demanded in a rush of anger that almost made her forget her fear.

Her uncle shook his head. His thin lips flickered with the beginnings of a rather unpleasant smile. "Temper, temper," he said. "Is that any way to welcome a long-lost member of your own family?"

Before she had the chance to reply, her mother rose from the couch. She swayed before the man, trembling and making little gurgling noises deep in her throat. After one last adoring look, her eyes rolled back in her head and her body slumped. Raden jumped from his chair and caught her just before she hit the floor. The half-eaten peach rolled from her fingers and struck the carpet with a soggy thud.

The half-eaten peach rolled from her fingers . . .

Later, it was the little things that stuck in Arica's mind. She recalled the way her mother's thick dark curls tumbled over her uncle's arm, and how a single strand became tangled around one of the buttons of his cloak. She recalled the hard glitter of satisfaction in his eyes as he spoke that one last time. And she remembered the way the world suddenly grew still, as if waiting with bated breath for what might happen next.

"Your father is as foolish as he is forgetful," his harsh voice informed her as he hoisted her mother higher. "No woman is worth giving up a kingdom for, not even one as beautiful as this."

Then with a final laugh and a swirl of his long,

black cloak, her uncle swept across the living room and out the doorway. Before she could even cry out he was down the hallway, through the front door and gone, carrying her mother away with him.

Then it became like one of those terrible nightmares she used to have when she was younger, where the faster she ran from danger, the slower she went. But this was real. She stumbled across the living room, bumped against a chair, nearly tripped on the rug, then staggered down the hallway. Thankfully the door was already open wide, for her panic-stiffened fingers would certainly have wasted precious moments fumbling with the knob. She ran out into the yard, waving and shouting, but it was only to empty air and a deserted street.

Raden and her mother had disappeared.

Arica stood on the sidewalk for a long, terrifying moment, staring up and down the road and trying to gain control of her runaway emotions. What she needed the most right now was a clear head and some calm, logical thinking. Hysterics would accomplish nothing except to give her uncle more time to get away. The first thing she had to do was figure out where he was going with her mother, and why.

Earth was not his home, although he often bragged about hunting here, and she had seen his many trophies. Other than that, he'd never said anything good about this place that she could remember. In fact, in the past, this world had been a danger to him. Before Arica found the *Book of Fairies*, too long a stay here would have made Raden forget his true nature and his magic. It had happened to Arica's own father. Once he had been heir to the throne of North Bundelag, sent here on a mission to find that country's lost fairies. But he had stayed too long and forgotten what he was. And Arica's beautiful, lively, stubborn, fully human mother never knew.

There was a chance she would, though, now that Arica and Wish had called the fairies home to Bundelag. Arica's heart thudded. Bundelag — that's where Raden was taking her mother. She was sure of it. And that meant he was headed for Grandmother's house and the crack between the worlds.

Arica dashed to the backyard where her bike was kept. Though it seemed to waste precious seconds, she knew that once she got going she'd be at Grandmother's faster this way. She skidded across the yard and down the street in a flurry of screeching tires and whirling pedals. She sailed over curbs and through ditches, skirted hedges and dodged people and cars. It seemed as if the journey lasted forever, but in reality it took her only a few minutes.

She leaped from her bike while it was still moving and let it go, hardly caring as it bounced and clattered across the cement driveway. She groped underneath the potted plant for the key that Grandmother always kept hidden for her, then scrambled up the porch steps.

In her panic, it took her three tries to insert the key into the lock. The key refused to turn. It took a long, agonizing moment for her to realize that the door was already unlocked. She flung it wide open and, not even pausing to pull the key back out, raced down the front hall, through the living room, and into Grandmother's kitchen.

Raden and her mother were nowhere in sight. But standing in a half circle around the dishwasher, facing her with their swords drawn, were half a dozen filthy, black-toothed, red-eyed trolls.

Chapter 2

It took Arica only a few seconds to realize there was no hope of getting anywhere near the crack, let alone through it and into the cellar.

In Bundelag, with a unicorn at her side and her father's sword in her hand, she might have had a chance of winning a fight with six armed trolls. But here on Earth she was just an ordinary girl with no magic and very little muscle to back her up.

However, that didn't mean she couldn't give it her best effort.

"Get out of my way!" she cried as she grabbed a steel frying pan from Grandmother's stove-top.

The trolls responded by lifting their swords higher and stepping closer. She shivered, slid back just a little, and waved the pan in front of her.

"My grandmother is the Fairy Queen of Bundelag!" she exclaimed. She allowed her voice to rise with just the right amount of indignation. "I have urgent business there! Let me through!"

The trolls muttered to each other in that clunky, garbled way they had of speaking that sounded like teeth clacking on rocks. As always, the magic that enabled her to understand troll speech kicked in, turning the words into English, though a slightly mangled version. Sometimes she wished she didn't understand them quite so well, especially when they spewed out insults, which was nearly all of the time. At the moment they were telling her that the only way she would get into Bundelag was over their dead bodies.

"Fine," she said, and flung the pan. She heard it bong against something hard — hopefully a thick troll skull — but didn't stop to check. Instead, she dashed through the living room, clenching her teeth to keep from howling in frustration. She slammed the door behind her, mentally apologizing to Grandmother, and yanked the key from the lock. Her eyes stung and her throat felt dry and raw. She had to get past the trolls and into Bundelag. But how? She needed help. She needed someone who could assist her in coming up with a plan, someone who had been to Bundelag before, had met her uncle, and understood what they were up against.

She needed her cousin Connor.

But as usual, there was a problem. Neither she nor Connor was old enough to drive a car. Maybe if she pleaded long and loud enough to his parents, one of them would give him a ride in from the farm. They were her aunt and uncle after all, and knew her well enough to recognize when she was truly desperate. And she was. Her mother was kidnapped, her father away on a business trip somewhere. And who knew where in two worlds Grandmother was? Arica didn't dare think about what would happen if Connor's parents refused. Back to her bike she dashed, hopped on, and sped for home to make the call.

Connor arrived three long, agonizing hours later. By that time Arica knew full well that Raden had the head start he needed. Her only hope was to get to the Fairy Village and enlist Grandmother's help in tracking him down. But first, she would have to fight her way past the trolls. She concocted a plan, in between bouts of pacing and hand-wringing, and then watched for her cousin through the window.

Arica dragged Connor inside before he even had the chance to knock. He looked a little frayed himself, for his glasses hung askew on his nose and his hair looked as if a small cyclone had recently circled his head. He settled on the sofa and squinted questioningly up at her through his bottle-bottom lenses.

"Sorry I took so long," he said. "I was helping Dad round up cattle. And he's been acting so odd lately, I don't like to bug him about anything unless it's absolutely necessary."

"Don't worry about it," she replied, and told her story.

"Oh, wow," he said when she was done. "This is bad. Really bad."

"Here's my plan," Arica said. She whipped out some objects that she'd recently dug from the closet and waved them under his nose.

Connor stared at one of them in horror. "A curtain rod!" he wailed, leaping to his feet. "You expect me to take on three or more armed trolls with a curtain rod! What are you thinking? The only way I'll get out of this in one piece is if they die laughing!" He paused, then added with a grin: "Maybe that's not such a bad plan after all."

Arica let that one pass. She was in no mood for jokes. "You only have to pretend to attack them with the curtain rod. As they run toward you, throw this curtain on top of them. By the time they get untangled, I'll be through the crack and you'll be safely back outside. Don't worry about the trolls following you. They'll be after me."

"Are you sure about that?"

"I'm sure. You're no threat to them."

"I'm taking that as a personal insult to my manhood," he said, still half-joking, though he looked more serious now.

"Don't," she said as she turned to go. "Just consider yourself lucky."

Ten minutes later they let themselves into Grandmother's house by the front door. The silence hung around them like a heavy cloak as they tiptoed down the hallway and through the living room. They paused beside the door to the kitchen. Beside her, Connor took a deep breath and squared his shoulders. Then, holding the curtain rod up in front of him and with the curtain rolled up under his other arm, he gave her a final nod and stepped through the doorway into the kitchen.

Arica waited impatiently, expecting at any moment to hear guttural shouts of surprise, the clang of swords striking against the metal rod, and the patter of running feet as the trolls scrambled after Connor. The seconds dragged by in silence. She remained where she was as long as she could stand it, then peeked cautiously around the edge of the door frame.

Connor had climbed up onto the counter and was peering behind Grandmother's fridge. The kitchen was empty. The trolls were nowhere in sight. In fact, now that she thought about it, they couldn't possibly be anywhere in the house. The disgusting odour of mouldy cheese and dirty socks that always accompanied them was gone. Obviously the trolls had returned to Bundelag.

"Well, that makes it easier," said Arica briskly. "Lock the door when you leave, will you, Connor? I'm not sure when I'll be back."

"What do you mean, you'll be back?" demanded Connor, poking his head behind the stove. (Could six trolls really cram into a space so small?) Satisfied that they weren't hidden there either, he turned toward her.

Arica shook her head. "I'm going to Bundelag, but you're not coming. It's *my* mother that he kidnapped, not yours. This could get very dangerous, even life-threatening. You don't know my uncle like I do. I'm not willing to risk your life, and that's what I'd be doing if I let you come."

At first Connor just stood there and blinked, as if she had socked him in the stomach and he couldn't quite catch his breath. She saw his hand clench into a fist. His eyes grew bright with something close to anger.

"You don't have the right to make that decision," he said. "My life belongs to me, and the risk is my choice, not yours."

Once again, Connor's new confidence had jumped up and bit Arica. Once he had been mild and predictable. Even just a few weeks ago, he'd have backed down beneath her glare and accepted her decision as the final one.

But since their recent journey into Bundelag — when he had helped her to outsmart Raden and bring back the lost *Book of Fairies* — a new Connor had begun to take the place of the quiet, timid boy she'd always known.

Silently, Arica looked at her cousin. The last thing she'd learned just before returning home from Bundelag was that Connor was half fairy like herself, and that his father, like her own, was a fairy lost on earth without any memory of his home or his magic. Connor didn't know any of this, for Grandmother hadn't as yet given Arica permission to tell him. But she suspected that deep down, somewhere below the level of his conscious thought, he had always known that there was something different about him.

Arica sighed, just so her cousin would realize how unbearably annoying she found all of this, then shrugged her shoulders.

"You're right," she admitted. "It's your life and I can't stop you from coming. But you've never seen Raden at his worst, and you haven't been kidnapped by trolls or nearly bitten to death by pfipers."

"It sounds like a marvellous adventure!" he exclaimed, and grinned again.

"You won't be saying that a while from now," she warned, "so quit gloating and come on. I'm in a hurry."

Connor followed close behind her as she stepped through the crack in Grandmother's floor. Together they tumbled down into the cellar, picked themselves up, brushed themselves off, and made their way through the passageway that led to Bundelag.

On previous visits Arica had been totally lost upon entering Bundelag, but she'd been here enough times now that she was beginning to learn one direction from the other. At least she thought she was. They had definitely been facing south when they came out of the tunnel, hadn't they? Or was it southeast? Oh, well. She didn't figure it mattered too much. She used to get quite worried when she came here, but not anymore. The unicorns always seemed to know when she returned, and she was confident that sooner or later either Wish or an elf would show up to guide her.

As it turned out, what showed up was Wish *and* an elf.

Arica and Connor had been fighting their way through the underbrush for about half an hour when they heard a voice call out to them from behind a clump of trees.

"You're going in the wrong direction!" it bellowed. "Keep on that way and you'll end up in the northern ice fields playing hide-and-seek with the wolves!"

A rush of joy went through Arica, and she laughed in spite of the pain and anxiety that burdened her. For if she wasn't mistaken, that gruff, grumbly voice could only belong to Nue the elf, and that tingle in her veins was because a unicorn was near. She dashed toward the place where the voice had come from at the same moment as Nue and Wish burst through the trees directly in front of her.

Nue was mounted on one of Grandmother's enormous grey stallions, and when the horse saw her right under its nose, it stopped suddenly so it wouldn't run her over. Nue, being hopelessly unskilled at almost everything, including riding, was unable to stop with the animal. As a result, he sailed over its left shoulder, arms and legs flailing, did a rather untidy mid-air flip, and landed face down in a pile of newly fallen leaves.

Then Wish bounded up, nickering with joy, and Arica flung her arms around her friend's neck. She buried her face in the silky, silver mane and laughed with pleasure and relief. Everything was better now that Wish was here. Together they would find her mother and break the spell that Raden had put upon her.

She pulled back from Wish and turned around just in time to see Connor drag Nue out of the leaves by one arm.

"Thank you, lad," said the chubby, rather grubby elf as he brushed himself off. One large leaf poked ridiculously up from his head like a lone feather. "A good and noble boy, just as I thought. I heard all about your last great adventure from the Fairy Queen herself! Indeed I did. I knew you had it in you, lad. Right from the first moment I met you, I knew. I said to myself, there is something special about that boy. Yes, indeed. You fought bravely at young Arica's side, I hear, and protected her against the many dangers of the South. Weren't you the one that realized the first *Book of Fairies* was a fake, and insisted upon returning for the real one? Clever young man! I'm not sure that even I could have seen through Raden's evil scheme. Although, I had a similar experience back when — "

"Nue!" Arica interrupted. If she didn't stop him, there was no telling how long he'd babble on. "I need to talk to the Fairy Queen right away! Something terrible has happened!"

Nue turned two large, sad eyes upon her. "Yes, brave Arica," he said. "The Fairy Queen will meet you at the Fairy Village."

"There's no time to go to the Fairy Village!" cried Arica. "You don't understand! I have to go after Raden! He stole my mother!"

Nue nodded unhappily. The leaf on his head waved at her like a friendly hand. "Let me explain, fearless Arica. The Fairy Queen has been watching Raden for some time. She knew when he sneaked back into North Bundelag. When her elves reported that he escaped through the crack to Earth, she arrived just in time to catch him as he returned."

"And then?" Arica managed to squeak out.

"The Fairy Queen saw that he had your mother with him. There were terrible words spoken. Fairy power thickened in the air until we elves could hardly breathe. Sparks snapped and flew." With those words, Nue paused and shivered. After a moment he continued: "When it was all over, Raden and his trolls departed, leaving your mother with us. The Fairy Queen has taken her to the Fairy Village where she will be safe."

"Why didn't you say so in the first place?" said Arica. "Let's go there now!" She took a few flying leaps, then halted. "Which way is the Fairy Village, anyway?"

That's when she felt Wish's satin-smooth nose against her hand and heard the grief-filled words whisper in her mind.

I'm sorry, True Arica, the unicorn said.

"Sorry?" Arica asked. "What are you sorry for, Wish?"

"You didn't give me time to finish explaining, courageous Arica," said Nue. "What I've been trying to tell you is that your mother is far from well. The poison Raden gave her is very strong. She has fallen into a deep sleep, and not even the Fairy Queen can wake her."

Chapter 3

Unfortunately, the quickest route to the Fairy Village took them right through the Badlands.

Connor had never experienced the Badlands before, and though he didn't complain, Arica got the feeling it would never rank high on his list of favourite vacation spots. There was nothing unusual in that, and she didn't blame him when he grew more silent and gloomy as the hours passed. The Badlands affected everyone that way. She had tried to warn him, of course, but this place was something you had to experience to fully understand.

They were surrounded by grey skies and ragged black hills. The soot rose up in dusty billows around them with every step that their mounts took. It settled on their necks and in their eyes and ears, entered their throats and nostrils in the air they breathed, and worked its gritty way into their shoes and clothes. To make matters worse, the heat was close to unbearable. Before long they were pouring with sweat, which mingled with the dust on their bodies until it felt caked on.

"I'd forgotten how much I hate this place," muttered Nue, wiping a grimy hand across his brow and leaving behind yet another smear.

"Not me," said Arica. "I recall the heat, the dust, and the wolf with perfect clarity. And except for the wolf, who hasn't turned up yet, they're every bit as bad as I remember."

"The wolf?" asked Connor, twisting around on the horse to stare back at her.

"You should get Nue to tell you about it," she suggested. That should help them to keep their minds off their discomfort for a while. Nue was always eager to tell a story — as eager as Connor was to hear one. In that aspect, they made perfect travelling companions.

"It happened just after brave Arica and the unicorn Wish visited the Fairy Village and received a message from the Fairy Queen to go and search for Raden . . . " Nue began.

Arica tried to pay attention, but she was unable to

focus on what he was saying, not even to correct the exaggerations that always crept in when Nue recounted an adventure. Her mind kept returning to her mother. And every time it did, her stomach rolled sickly inside of her and her eyes stung with tears waiting to fall. Maybe if she had done something different, things wouldn't have turned out this way. If she had arrived home just a few minutes sooner, she might have prevented her mother from eating that peach. Or a few minutes sooner still, and she might have kept her uncle from getting through the door at all.

Arica forced her mind off the past and into the

The soot rose up in dusty billows around them with every step that their mounts took.

present. The Fairy Queen must have considered the situation a very grave one to take Arica's mother — a full-blooded human — inside the hidden Fairy Village. It was a place that even the elves were rarely invited to enter. If only they could get to the Fairy Village more quickly! At times like this Arica found travel by horseback (and unicornback) agonizingly slow, and wished heartily that someone in Bundelag had invented cars. Even a motorbike or two would help. But then it wouldn't be Bundelag anymore, only a copy of the mad, mechanical world that was her home.

Anyway, she had to admit that in her present

state of mind, even travel by jet plane would have seemed slow. In fact, with Nue and Connor astride the grey stallion, and her riding Wish, by Bundelag standards they were making pretty good time. Sometime tomorrow (if they made it through the night unscathed), they'd be crossing the Black River.

Much as Arica wanted to be out of the Badlands, she dreaded that crossing. The Black River was an oily, muddy thing, filled with an evil kind of consciousness that howled inside her head and filled her thoughts with dreadful fantasies and fears. She knew the river would affect Connor in the same way, though elves and unicorns were immune. She'd long ago discovered that in this land, rivers and fairies seemed to be tied together in some inexplicable way.

The time dragged by as she sorted and resorted all of these problems in her mind, and the coming of night found them still well within the border of the Badlands. They camped with their backs to a bluff, huddled around a tiny fire beneath a clump of sickly trees. The night turned out to be as cold and bitter as the day was hot. Thankfully Arica had remembered to grab the pack she always kept hidden at her grandmother's house, for without her flashlight and matches they'd have had very little light and no heat. Nue couldn't conjure any elven fire here, nor Wish set logs to blazing with a touch of her horn.

Drusa and Perye, the two elves that had accompanied her on that very first journey through the Badlands, had told her that magic didn't work here — even the magic of unicorns.

After talking it over, they decided Connor would take the first watch, Nue the second, and Arica the last. If there was one thing they all agreed upon, it was that they shouldn't all go to sleep at once and leave themselves open to attack. One never knew who or what might turn up in this place.

At some point during the night, Arica's grandfather visited her in a dream.

She knew she was dreaming, yet he seemed so real and near it was almost as if she could reach out and tweak the whiskers on his chin. Robust and cheerful, he floated down beside her, settling only half a metre above the ground. He patted his pockets in search of his pipe, gave up when he couldn't find it, then leaned back in the air and peered at her from beneath his scrub-brush eyebrows.

"Hello, Grandfather," she said, smiling up at him. "When will I deserve a real visit? It seems to me that the last time you visited me here in the Badlands, it was also in a dream."

"This is as real as the visit will get," the old fairy replied. "The fact is, only the very bad or the very brave enter the Badlands. I am neither."

"How did you get inside my dream?" Arica

wondered. "You must be using magic. But as everyone knows, magic doesn't work here."

"Of course it doesn't," he said. "That's why I have to hurry. I can feel my power draining away even as we speak."

"What did you come here to tell me?" her dreamself inquired cheerfully.

Grandfather stood, still in mid-air. His body was already beginning to fade. In fact, her whole dream was starting to dissolve into nothing, as dreams often do.

"You're in danger," Grandfather warned, his voice already sounding somewhat hollow and far away. "You must wake up and resume your journey — now. Ega is near. Beware of Ega . . . " Then Grandfather and her dream melted into darkness.

Arica had no idea how much longer she slept, but the next thing she knew, two hands gripped her by the shoulders and shook her, none too gently. A voice shouted in her ear. She groaned and tried to push the annoyance away, but it only grew more insistent. At last her sleep-dimmed brain recognized Nue. She groaned. It must be her turn to stand watch. As she attempted to pry open her uncooperative eyes, she heard a soft nicker and felt Wish's warm breath blow past her cheek.

Wake up, True Arica, the unicorn said. *There is danger here.*

Her memory of Grandfather's visit and of his warning came back in a rush that drove her upright, her eyes suddenly wide and staring. She peered around in alarm but all she saw was Nue's homely, haggard face just centimetres from her own, the gentle eyes of the unicorn, and beyond that, the circle of trees blanketed in darkness.

Oh, why hadn't she made herself get up after her dream, and warn the others? Now it was too late. For just beyond the reach of their tiny, flickering fire she saw three shadows detach themselves from all the other nameless shadows of the night and drift silently towards them.

Connor stirred beneath his blanket as if he sensed that something was amiss, though he still slept. Grandmother's stallion moved restlessly nearby. Wish snorted and tossed her head, her dark eyes glinting with alarm.

Nue turned on the flashlight.

Arica had always wondered what female trolls looked like, for in all her dealings with Raden's trolls, she had only ever seen males. But if she'd been given the choice of a time and place to meet one, the middle of a moonless night in the heart of the Badlands wouldn't have been her first pick.

They were without doubt the ugliest creatures she had ever seen. All three of them were short and thickly built, with sharp hooked noses, thin cruel lips pulled tightly back from stained brown teeth, and small red eyes. Their skin was the colour of clay and marred by warts and the occasional large mole. Their hair couldn't have seen a comb in the last month, and their dresses were little more than rags. But any compassion Arica might have felt for their wretched condition was stifled when they began to jabber, for their harsh, high voices shrilled in the quiet night like claws scraping over stone.

"A unicorn!" cried one of them with glee. She was by far the strongest looking of the three and, judging by the way the others let her take the lead, seemed to be the one in charge. Her eyes glittered with greed as they fell upon Wish. "It's been such a long time," she crooned. "Come to me, my lovely."

Arica had no idea what she meant by such a remark, but thankfully Wish stayed where she was.

"You can't have her," Arica said to the troll. "She's not yours for the taking. She's my friend, and she's staying with me."

The troll cackled. It was a rattly, joyless sound. "What makes you think I care?" she said. "And what makes you think you can stop me?"

Over by the fire, Connor looked as though he was still happily dreaming beneath his one thin blanket. But she couldn't help but notice that he (and it) had moved about half a metre farther from the fire since the last time she looked. He clearly had some sort of plan in mind, for his hand had come to rest beside a fist-sized rock.

"I'm not interested in you, elf," the troll said to Nue. "You're free to go. But these two human children intrigue me. I can smell fairy blood all over the place. No doubt there's a fascinating story behind all of this."

"I won't leave without my friends," said Nue stubbornly.

"Admirable, but stupid," she replied.

"Could this be Ega?" Arica wondered, remembering her dream, then realized with alarm that she had spoken her thoughts out loud.

The blood-red eyes turned upon her. "How do you know my name?"

At that same moment, Nue jumped. He'd been keeping the flashlight beam low during most of the conversation. Suddenly he shone the light right in the head troll's face and cried: "I know who you are! You're Ega the enchantress!"

"Put that thing out!" Ega howled, throwing her arm up in front of her eyes. "Do you have any brains in that melon-sized skull of yours?" She swooped forward and yanked the flashlight from his hand, peered at it, then flicked it off and on again. Suddenly she twisted around and aimed a kick at one of her companions, who had the misfortune of standing too near. "Bring me the girl's sack! I want to see what other magic trinkets she has!"

Apparently Connor considered this as his cue, for the next moment he took the rock in his hand and sent it hurtling toward Ega's head.

Arica had to give the troll credit — stolid and square as she was, there was nothing wrong with her reflexes. At the last instant she saw the rock and ducked. It sailed over top of her, so close it might have cut a swath through the tangle on her head. The female troll standing behind her wasn't so lucky — she looked up just in time to catch it right between her beady red eyes. She toppled like an uprooted tree.

It was too late to turn back now. For one brief moment Arica wished that she had her father's sword. Although its magic would not have worked here in the Badlands, she might have at least sheared a few hairs off those ugly chins. And the odds had improved quite a lot in the last few seconds. It was now three against two in their favour — five against two counting Wish and the stallion, though it wasn't likely that Grandmother had trained the horse to fight.

But Ega had clearly realized the same thing. The troll raised her arms, and out of her mouth burst a shriek that raised dust clouds and rattled stones. All Arica could do was stand and watch in disbelief as the night suddenly came alive with answering caws and the beating of enormous wings. Then before they even had the chance to fight or flee, dozens of huge black birds swooped down upon them.

Chapter 4

"I thought magic didn't work in the Badlands," said Connor as he scowled at the birds.

He, Arica and Nue were sitting with their backs against a tree, guarded by a group of rather vicious-looking ravens. At least that's what Nue said they were. Where Arica came from, ravens weren't usually the size of swans, with beaks like pruning shears. The trolls sat some distance away, gobbling up everything in sight. They had eaten all the granola bars, Smarties, and beef jerky Arica had brought from home and were starting on Nue's rations, but with much less enthusiasm. All his pack contained was the usual North Bundelag fare of dry biscuits, hunks of old cheese, and a few small, sour apples.

"It isn't her magic that brings them," Nue explained. "It's just Ega. For some reason, ravens like her."

"That's probably because they're just as beaky and sharp-clawed as she is," said Connor with a shudder.

Arica turned toward her friends. "Grandfather was here just a little while ago," she said. "He warned me that Ega was coming. But I didn't wake up in time."

"When did your grandfather come?" asked Connor, his eyes brightening. Connor was always eager to see Grandfather. He'd been fascinated by the fairy elder right from the first moment they met. "Was I sleeping?"

"No, I was," she said, then giggled at his look of confusion.

Connor frowned at her for a moment, then gave up trying to figure it out and turned his attention to Nue. "Just before the ravens came, you seemed to recognize Ega. Have you seen her before? Who is she, anyway?"

"She's every elf child's worst nightmare," Nue replied. "She's well known among my people because it's so rare for a troll to have magic. Trolls without magic are bad enough, but with it — well, I can't even begin to tell you how scary that is for an elf child. I can remember my mother saying, 'Nue, if you don't stop telling lies, Ega the enchantress will come while you're sleeping and steal you away!' I can tell you that I lay awake wide-eyed and trembling for many a long night, listening for the creaking of the door."

Arica tried to imagine this younger version of Nue. Of course he would have big terrified eyes, a thatch of tangled hair, and feet too large for his shoes. She smiled at the picture in her mind.

They spent the next few hours trying, without much success, to get some sleep. Then just as the sun reached up to touch the darkness, bringing with it another dusty dawn, she looked over to where Wish and the stallion were standing and saw that Wish was no longer there.

At first she thought that Ega had hidden Wish somewhere, or ordered the ravens to carry her off or some other terrible thing. But as soon as Ega opened her mouth, she dismissed that theory.

"So you sent your little pet away, did you?" screeched the troll as she leaned close, her face contorted with rage. Globs of spit flew from her mouth and spattered over Arica's cheeks and chin. "You won't get away with this!"

"I didn't send her anywhere," Arica shouted back, wanting desperately to kick the meddling old bag in the shin, or better yet, to stuff her mouth with a rag.

"You're lying!"

"She never lies," piped up Nue. "Don't you know anything about Arica and her unicorns? Why, she's honest and brave! Let me tell you about the time — "

"Be quiet!" the troll shrieked. She whacked Nue on the side of his head with her hand. Then, shouting with rage, she stomped through the fire. Sparks flew in every direction. She grabbed a twig and flung it at Arica, then kicked up a spray of dirt into Connor's face. The howling and clumping continued for a full minute longer while the birds flapped and flopped around her in alarm. Finally the tirade subsided to a few scuffles and some quiet mumbling.

"Well," Connor muttered to Arica, "I'd say the female trolls are proving to be just as disgusting and ill-mannered as the males."

After a hasty breakfast of biscuits and cheese for the trolls, and nothing for the rest of the company, Ega shoved them to their feet and informed them it was time to leave.

"That way," she said, pointing a plump, black-nailed finger toward the southeast. "Isn't it convenient that we both want to go in the same direction? I guess some things are just meant to be." The cackle that followed made Arica's nerves jangle, but she managed to hold her tongue.

She had no way of telling how long they walked, for the sun was lost in a hot, hazy sky and its path was impossible to trace. It might have gone easier if they had been allowed to ride, but the trolls' attitude was that if they couldn't ride the creature, then neither could anyone else. Grandmother's stallion had shied every time the trolls attempted to mount him, so they gave up on the whole idea and left it to trail along behind. The hours dragged at a snail's crawl, and time became a blurry nightmare of heat and hunger and thirst and pain. And of course, they were surrounded at all times by dozens of vicious, cawing birds.

And then they came to the Black River.

If Arica had any doubts about Connor being half fairy, they were immediately swept away by the look she saw on his face as they drew near to the sludgy, slough-like mess that passed for water here in the Badlands. At least she understood what was going on — that this was just one of those things about being a fairy. But poor Connor had no idea who he really was or what was happening here, and thought, no doubt, that he was losing his mind. Even Arica had to admit the river's voice was louder and a lot worse than she remembered. Or perhaps it was simply that she had succeeded at not remembering. Before long, it took all her strength not to scream along with it.

When they finally slopped their filthy way to the other side, her cousin's face was as white as the moons of Bundelag and his eyes like two of their darkest craters. She saw him stumble up the far bank and collapse beside a clump of bushes, too shaken to take another step. She yearned to help him understand what was happening to him, but of course there was nothing she could do without her grandmother's permission. Perhaps Grandmother wanted to tell him about his fairy father herself, or maybe she felt that he wasn't ready to handle it yet. Whatever the reason, Arica didn't dare take any chances, so she remained silent.

The trolls yanked Connor to his feet and they went on. Later they stopped to rest beside a wagon-sized boulder so the trolls could squabble over the last few morsels of cheese and apple. The argument proved to be a brief one, however, for Ega just slapped the faces of the other two and ordered them to hand over their share. Arica preferred not to watch their childish squabbling. She had a sip of the water Nue had managed to keep hidden, then collapsed with her back against the rock, so weak and weary she could hardly focus her aching eyes. She stared off into the distance, yearning for root beer on ice, thick-crust pizza, a bubble bath and a toothbrush, preferably in that order.

Gradually, through her fog of exhaustion, she perceived that they were now within a hundred metres of the border between the Badlands and the rest of

North Bundelag. Off in the distance the blue skies of Bundelag beckoned to her, bright with sunshine and flecks of silver cloud. If only she could be like Ega's birds and just launch herself upward to sunlight and freedom. And that made her think of Wish. She had worried all day long about the unicorn, wondering where she was and what she was doing, and trying not to fear the worst. She hoped desperately that the unicorn had made it this far.

Then, because that was the way with her and the unicorns, all of a sudden she knew.

I'm right behind you, True Arica, said a voice inside her head.

It took all of the will power she possessed not to scream in joy and fling herself around.

"I'm so glad you're back!" she whispered as she stood. "Where have you been?"

I didn't tell you my plan, explained Wish, *for when the bad troll people asked you where I was, you would have told them the truth.*

Arica was startled. When she had first come to Bundelag, Wish had been a colt, simple and playful and free. Despite all they'd accomplished together since, Arica still thought of Wish that way. Now, she saw that Wish had grown up. It made her sad, some-how.

"I could have refused to answer," she said.

They might have hurt you.

Arica nodded. "I can see you thought things over very carefully," she admitted, "and you're probably right. But what is this plan you didn't tell me about?"

This is where the bad land ends, said Wish. *I hurried here to wait. I have my magic again. Take it and attack your enemy. Free yourself now, while you can still surprise her.*

Just then, the ravens screeched as if a bird-eating tiger had just leaped into their midst. Ega heard the uproar and her head whipped around. Her eyes widened, and she raised her arm. With a sinking heart, Arica realized that the troll woman's magic had also returned. The enchantress flicked her wrist and a ball of yellow light hurtled down upon them.

It took Arica only an instant to pull the power she needed from Wish's horn. She felt it rush over her skin and race all clean and bubbly through her veins. Her bones sang with the joy of it as she shaped a tiny, glittering egg of blue between her palms and sent it soaring high above her head. It struck Ega's yellow ball and exploded in a blast of light and sound that rattled teeth and hurtled rocks and dust into the air.

Ega's two companions dived for cover. Nue and Connor flung up their arms and dashed behind the rock. Ravens shrieked and floundered around them. Another flash of yellow came at her, and then another. She drove them both back. Again and

Again and again she countered the troll, blow for blow.

again she countered the troll, blow for blow. At last they paused and stood facing one another while the sky rained dirt around them and the air howled with half-spent fury.

"You're no match for me, little girl!" screeched Ega through the din. "If you play with fire, you'll get burned!"

"I could say the same," shouted Arica.

Three more rounds came at her. She drove them back, but it was becoming harder now. She could feel a gradual weakening of Wish's power.

"Let us go," she said to the troll. "That's all I ask."

"Never!" Ega spat out, and raised her arms again.

Then through the haze of dust and wind Arica saw an enormous wolf lope silently toward them. Her heart lurched. This was the same black wolf that had saved their lives during an earlier journey through the Badlands. Surely he would not harm them now? She turned her attention back to the troll and was amazed to see Ega's face frozen in a grimace of rage . . . mixed with a trace of fear. Her mouth wagged as she tried to speak. With an outcry and a flapping of powerful wings, her ravens rose in flight and disappeared.

"Leave us alone, Blackthorn," the enchantress shrilled in a tearful voice. "This has nothing to do with you."

The wolf snarled. He had teeth as long as kitchen

knives and a tongue the size of a dinner plate. Arica bet he could swallow a troll in one easy gulp. His eyes glowed red. They were even fiercer than Ega's.

"You have no right to do this," the enchantress whined.

Blackthorn scratched at the dirt with his paw. A growl rose from deep within his throat. His tongue lolled. Saliva dripped. He took another step forward.

Ega gave one last shriek of fury and stomped away. Arica stared after her in amazement and relief, hardly daring to believe that they were free of her at last. She watched with great delight as the troll scurried off into the distance, while her two companions, leaving all their belongings behind, scrambled to catch up. When at last Arica turned to thank the wolf for rescuing them, he had already disappeared.

Chapter 5

They arrived at the Fairy Village just as the sun sank wearily beneath a gold and crimson sky.

Or rather, they arrived at the probable location of the Fairy Village. For there was no village to be seen, only a pathway of flat brown stones that ran through a grassy field, arched across a small bridge, wound down a slope to a sandy beach and abruptly ended, just as futilely as it had begun.

But the meadow where the exhausted travellers stood was not empty, as it had been last time Arica was here. An army of elves had set up camp, right in the middle.

"I guess I forgot to tell you about this," Nue said

when he saw Arica's surprise.

Two of the elves had noticed their arrival and were hurrying in their direction. Nue squinted at them for a moment, then yelped with glee and darted off through the grass. It only took Arica a few seconds longer to recognize the pair of elves and then she also took off running, practically on Nue's heels. Wish, always eager for some fun, whinnied and bounded after her. Connor, gawking around, didn't notice right away that he was alone. When he did, he let out an indignant yell and rushed to catch up.

"My dear nephew Perye!" Nue was exclaiming even as they ran. "And my beloved niece Drusa! I'm so happy to see you again! You wouldn't believe the trouble we ran into on our way here. Nothing that courageous Arica, her noble cousin and her fine unicorn couldn't handle — with my help, of course. But still, what a journey! Ega the enchantress captured us! And we learned that the wolf who has twice saved me and brave Arica in the dreaded Badlands is named Blackthorn — "

Nue's prattle was cut off suddenly as Drusa grabbed him and smothered him with a hug. Then Arica could no longer see what was happening because Perye's arms were around her and her face was squished against his shoulder. Then it was Connor's turn, and what followed next was a flurry of embraces and back-thumping so intense that it left everyone pink-faced and breathless. At one point during the confusion, Arica saw that Connor's glasses had been pushed off his nose and dangled foolishly down his cheek, snagged by one ear. The boy was too delighted to notice. In the meantime Nue was hopping up and down and whooping. Wish's horn had started to crackle with little blue lights, like a birthday cake sparkler. Finally Arica pulled back to catch her breath and to try to restore some order to the situation.

"What's going on here?" she asked Perye when she could be heard again. She gestured toward the rows of tents, the fire pits, and the numerous small hobbled horses that were standing just beyond them.

"The Fairy Queen set this up as a meeting place for new recruits," explained Perye. "Our army is growing daily, which is a good thing. In our last battle we only just held off the human invaders, and their army is still camped in South Bundelag near our border. But never mind about that. You must be tired from your long journey. Your grandmother is expecting you in the Fairy Village. And," he added, his green eyes sad, "you're probably anxious to see your mother."

The unexpected sympathy made Arica's eyes sting with unshed tears. She turned away so he wouldn't notice. "See you soon, then," she said. She took a few steps, then realized that although Wish was following her as she should, Connor wasn't. She stopped and turned.

"Come on, Connor," she said, beckoning.

Connor stepped forward, and Arica heard Perye gasp. Over Connor's shoulder, she saw the elf frown, and even Drusa look concerned. Her cousin hesitated.

"I thought only fairies were allowed in the Fairy Village," he said. "And unicorns, of course. Maybe I should just stay here with Perye and Drusa and Nue. I — I'm only human, you know."

"Some humans are allowed," Arica said impatiently. "My mother is there."

"That's a special case. Your mother is hurt and was brought to Bundelag against her will."

Arica sighed in frustration. "Connor," she said, "do you trust me?"

He stared at her, looking confused and a little hurt that she would even ask. "Of course I do!"

"Then trust me on this one. I know the Fairy Queen wants you to come."

"All right," he agreed, his forehead still wrinkled with doubt. "But if I get into trouble, I'm going to blame it all on you."

"Fair enough," she said, inwardly sighing in relief. And along the stone pathway she led him, through the grassy field, across the bridge and down the slope towards the beach and the sparkling sea beyond.

With his first steps on the bridge, Connor gasped in amazement and gripped her arm. She understood his surprise, for it wasn't so long ago that she'd seen the Fairy Village appear for the very first time. It dazzled her all over again with its springs of clear water that caught the last rays from the setting sun and glittered like liquid crystal. Without speaking, she nudged Connor and pointed back the way they had come. The camp, the elves, and the horses were all gone, and in their place were the many brightly coloured cottages and flowers of the Fairy Village.

Entranced, Connor looked all around him, following the streams with his eyes as they spilled over stones and wound their way through gardens full of flowers that danced softly in the evening breeze.

"Oh, wow," said Connor.

"Is that all you know how to say?" Arica asked, holding back a giggle. "Come on. Let's find Grandmother."

They hadn't gone much further when it was Arica's turn to stop and stand gawking with her mouth wide open. Could this be the same Fairy Village she remembered? The beauty of the place hadn't changed — the hedges and lawns were the same brilliant green, and the Fairy Queen's castle loomed over it all like a sentinel carved of stone. But now Arica saw children popping out from behind those hedges and romping barefoot across those

The beauty of the place hadn't changed . . .

lawns. And the cottages were no longer empty and silent and dark. Men and women were lighting lamps in the windows, peering at her through curtains and slipping in and out of doorways. She felt a thrill of joy run through her. She and Wish had called the fairies, and they had started to come home.

She came out of her reverie just in time to see Connor and Wish disappear around a bend. As she was about to dash after them, a voice called out her name.

She turned. The voice belonged to a man she had never seen before. He had curly red hair and a round kind face that looked as though it had done a lot of smiling over the years. It was smiling now.

"My name is Tansley," the man said. "I saw you with the boy and the unicorn and I knew you must be the Fairy Queen's granddaughter. She told us how you helped to restore our memories, and I wanted to thank you."

"You're welcome," Arica replied, accepting his offered hand. "It was no big deal." She paused, remembering the robbers, the dungeon, and fleeing for her life from Haggdorn and Raden. "I take that back," she said. "It *was* a big deal. But you're welcome, anyway."

He let go of her hand, gave her a final nod of gratitude, and turned away. She stopped him with a question.

"What was it like to finally remember after all those years?" she asked. "When Wish and I called the fairies home, I wasn't sure it would work at all, let alone how. Now I'm wondering. Do you mind telling me?"

Tansley shook his head. His smile returned even bigger than ever, though she hadn't thought that was possible. "I don't mind," he said. "All of the fairies I talked to had an experience similar to mine. At first we felt unsettled, like we should be doing something or going somewhere, but we didn't quite know what or where. Then we started to remember little things. For example, I kept looking for another moon, though logic told me there had only ever been one. After a while we remembered whole blocks of time past. Before long, we had pieced our lives back together. At that point, we started finding each other, using newspapers and the Internet. Then we started looking for the cracks — those of us who were free to go, that is. Many chose to stay behind because of their ties with humans."

Arica nodded. "I know all about that," she said, half to herself.

Tansley continued. "Some found their way to your grandmother's house, and the one crack that was still open. But most of us were faced with cracks tightly closed by ourselves or others of our kind." Tansley shook his head, rueful, but still smiling.

"We'd done our jobs well, before your world took our memories away."

"How did you get through, then?" asked Arica.

Tansley's eyes grew bright. "With the return of our memories came the ability to use our magic again, and so we reopened the cracks."

She stared at him in dismay. "But they can only be closed from the Earth side!" she cried. "If you opened them and came through, they're still open! Now there's the risk that more humans will enter Bundelag!"

He nodded. "There's always that risk," he admitted. "But try not to worry. Those fairies that remained back on Earth closed the cracks behind the rest of us. A few cracks have been left open, but those are carefully guarded."

Arica heaved an inner sigh of relief. "How many of you came back?" she asked.

Now Tansley's smile dimmed. "Not enough," he said soberly. "Many of the cottages are still empty. Some of it can't be helped — many of our people went to Earth right after the Great War, which was over four hundred years ago. Those fairies lived out their lives on Earth and died. The ones returning now are those who went to Earth recently — within the last forty years or so. And of course . . . "

"What?" asked Arica.

"Well, you've seen the children, haven't you?"

Arica nodded.

"It's surprising how many of us met and married, Earthside, without knowing each other's true natures," said Tansley. "When we came to Bundelag, our children came, too. But how many grown-up children of fairy parents are Earthside still, confused and lost with no one to guide them home? This and the war with South Bundelag are the matters that occupy us constantly."

"I'm sorry," said Arica, "Life in Bundelag is probably harder now than it was when you left."

"That's correct," Tansley said. He touched her shoulder in a gesture of farewell. "Don't look so sad, young Arica. Despite our worries, this is a wonderful time for our people, and many good things are about to happen. But never mind — I've delayed you long enough. You'd better hurry and catch up with your friends now, before you lose them altogether!"

A few minutes later she found Wish and Connor waiting in the shade of a tree at the path's edge, and together they made their way through the bustling village and on up the road that led to the Fairy Queen's castle. When they drew near to it she saw that the drawbridge was down, the gate thrown wide open, and Doron, the Keeper of the Village, was stepping forward to meet them.

Chapter 6

Doron was ancient and gnarled, thin as a reed, and his voice was the sound of dry grass brushed by wind. But the handshake he offered them was firm, and there was magic shining from his eyes.

"Welcome, True One," he said to Arica. He turned and lowered his head in respect to the unicorn. "It's good to see you again, young Wish. And Connor, I've heard so much about you — all of it good. It's a pleasure to finally meet you. Follow me, and I'll take you to the Fairy Queen."

As they fell into step behind him, the anxiety Arica had been trying not to feel about her mother welled up inside of her. She forced herself to consider the problems before her. Mother was very ill and probably not even aware of where she was. Grandmother would have tried everything to counteract the poison, which meant that it was most likely a very rare and deadly one. But Arica had brought Wish, and she firmly believed that the magic of a unicorn would succeed where everything else had failed. It simply had to.

They followed Doron into the Great Hall. Seated at the massive oak and ebony table with a book in her hands was Grandmother, the Fairy Queen of Bundelag. She put down the book when she saw them, stood, and glided forward, holding out her hands in welcome.

Arica rushed forward, and as Grandmother's strong warm arms pulled her close, all of the pain and horror of the last few days came crashing down upon her. She felt the wall of protection she had built around her emotions begin to crumble, like a teetering stack of sticks. With one quick intake of breath she cried, "Where is my mother?" And then she burst into tears.

After a while she realized that Grandmother had pushed her onto a chair and was wiping her face with a cloth that felt like silk and smelled like the roses outside the castle gate. The warm air blowing on her neck must be coming from Wish, and that had to be Connor patting her awkwardly on the shoulder. She took the cloth from Grandmother and wiped her nose, hiccuped in a rather unladylike manner, and then bravely raised her eyes to theirs.

"I'm fine," she assured them all. "Really I am."

Doron returned then, and Connor and Arica fell on the supper he'd brought like the starving travellers they were. Wish was escorted away to her own meal and rest by a pair of obviously delighted fairy children. At Grandmother's insistence, Arica put aside her cares for the evening and joined Connor in exploring the castle and picking their rooms for the night. Doron gave them some comfortable nightshirts, taking away their travel-stained clothes for washing, and then the cousins indulged themselves in some wild bed-jumping, something forbidden to both of them back at home.

They slept long and deep that night. Grandmother joined them at the table in the Great Hall after a late breakfast. Arica greeted her with joy. "Everything will be all right, now," she explained in a rush of words. "Wish's magic will cure my mother. I just know it. If we can call the fairies home, then somehow, with Wish and me and the *Book of Fairies* working together, we can make my mother well. Then I'll take her home."

Grandmother shook her head, looking strangely sad. Silence fell, thick with tension and words waiting to be spoken. A few thudding heartbeats later

Grandmother spoke, but she seemed to flinch inwardly with every sound she uttered.

"The unicorns have already tried to heal your mother," she explained. "Song and Light arrived here just yesterday and offered their help, but their magic had no effect. Neither did any of my own herbs or spells. The poison is one that Raden brewed up himself, and only he has the antidote. He told me that he'll give it to me only if I step down as Queen of North Bundelag and turn the ruling of the country over to him."

All of Arica's hopes crumbled like a fortress built of sand. "I'll go after him!" she cried. "I'll get the antidote even if I have to steal it!"

The faces around her grew grey and grim. Grandmother's head shook in sorrow. Doron's eyes could not meet hers. The queen spoke again. Her voice was like the soft sad whisper of dying leaves.

"If we steal it, Raden will have the excuse he needs to make an outright attack on me and my elves. When the country is sufficiently weakened by civil war, the South will come in and conquer us."

"We can't let my mother sleep forever!" But Arica knew, even as the words left her mouth, that if Grandmother gave Raden what he wanted, it would mean the destruction of North Bundelag, the loss of countless lives, and the enslavement of an entire race of elves. But worst of all, it would mean the end of her beloved unicorns.

"I need some time alone to think," she said, and ran through the doorway without looking back.

Arica lost track of the time, then, for the castle garden was such a beautiful and peaceful place that it almost made her forget to be miserable. After thinking things over for a while, she decided there was no good solution to the difficulty that she faced. One life — no matter how important it was to her — wasn't worth the sacrifice of an entire country full of innocent people. Even her mother would agree with that. In fact, she could see her mother's face in her mind, full of loving firmness, reminding her to always do what was right and honourable.

Why did right and honourable feel so awful?

After a while Wish joined her in the garden. The place was a unicorn's heaven, for flowers and butter-flies abounded. Wish nibbled at one and pursued the other, doing a great deal of chasing and very little catching. As a matter of fact the butterflies didn't seem to take her seriously, but teased her by tickling her ears and nose with their wings. It was clear that they knew a big goof when they saw one.

"You silly girl," Arica giggled, her heavy heart lifting just a fraction. "Come here and give me a kiss."

Wish pranced over, briefly nuzzled her cheek, and took off through the bushes again. When Arica finally turned back, she saw the Fairy Queen and

Connor stepping up to join her among the roses. Connor immediately flopped down beside her on the ground. Grandmother declined the spot of grass that Arica offered and instead picked out a flat rock nearby. The strain of these last few hours showed in the tired lines around her eyes and in the slow, almost pained way she moved.

But as usual, she was more worried about others than herself. "Are you feeling any better?" Grandmother asked Arica with concern.

"A bit," she admitted. "The garden has helped to clear my thoughts. I realize the unicorns did the best they could, and so did you. That's all anyone can do."

"Those are wise words," Grandmother said with a smile. "Do you believe *you* did the best you could?"

For one long moment, Arica gazed into her grandmother's eyes, and thought about that first agonizing time after Raden had taken her mother, when she herself couldn't stop thinking about what might have been. How did Grandmother know so much about her, without being told? At last, Arica grinned. "All right," she said. "You win."

"That's my girl," said the Fairy Queen. She rose from her rock and stepped forward to take Arica's hand. "Come. It's time for you to see your mother."

Arica's impression of the room was one of windows filled with sunlight and blue sky, and white lace curtains that fluttered in the breeze like fairies' wings. But fairies didn't have wings, and the beautiful room had a bed, and lying in that bed was her mother, still and pale as death.

She fell to her knees at the bedside and took her mother's hand in her own. Hope swelled inside her so suddenly that it hurt, for her mother's skin was still warm to the touch. She kissed the ashen cheek, then pressed her face against the quilts and closed her eyes.

She stayed that way for a very long time.

"I'll help you, Mother," she whispered. "I promise I will help you."

Later she, Connor, and Grandmother ate their dinner at the table in the Great Hall. Doron had prepared a meal of fish chowder, deliciously seasoned, to which a variety of fresh vegetables had been added. He served it with warm biscuits, honey and apple cider so icy cold that it burned as it went down.

Arica tried her best to do the meal justice, but in spite of her new resolve not to blame herself, her stomach felt queasy and rolled in complaint every time she raised her spoon. All she could think of was her mother's still, white face and the dark, silky fan of her hair against the pale pillow.

"I'll do better tomorrow," she promised when Grandmother frowned at her barely touched food.

Doron made no comment when he took it away, but he squeezed her shoulder gently as he went by.

After they were finished eating, Grandmother leaned back in her chair as though she planned to stay there for a while, and fixed her gaze on Connor. Arica groaned inwardly, for it seemed Grandmother was settling in to give them (or at least him) a long and serious lecture about something.

"I'll start my story at the beginning," she announced without preamble. "Five hundred years ago Bundelag time, during an epidemic of the Black Death on Earth, some humans discovered the cracks between the worlds and fled here for safety. At first they were welcomed, then conflict sprung up, which in a hundred years hardened into war. That war between the descendants of those early refugees and our ancestors — the Great War, we call it — resulted in a great deal of killing, much loss of magic, and a complete separation of the humans from the elves and fairies.

"All the while, people still kept trickling in through the cracks between our worlds, despite the fact that we had closed them from our side. The fairies that ruled Bundelag decided that cracks had to be closed on the Earth side, once and for all, in order to protect the country from further invasion. A host of fairy folk were sent to do that, then return through one remaining crack. But — "

"Oh, wow," said Connor, unable to contain himself. "This is a cool story. Did you know about this, Arica?"

Grandmother frowned at the interruption and continued. "As I was saying, something went wrong, and the fairies didn't return. Gradually, over the centuries, more and more fairies left, determined to find the lost ones. By the time we had figured out the problem, the only fairies left in all of Bundelag were Raden, myself and my husband, and Doron, the Keeper of the Village."

She paused, and Connor jumped in. "What was the problem?" he asked.

"We now know that once on Earth, fairies lose all memory of their former home and their magic — some quickly, some slowly — and become like ordinary humans," answered Grandmother. "Until recently, that was the way things were. Then Arica arrived, and met Wish. Things started to change. Because you and Arica found this," — she pointed to the *Book of Fairies* lying beside her place at the table — "the lost fairies have started to return. Which brings me to the most important thing I have to say."

Grandmother turned her full attention to Connor. There was a short silence, while Connor squirmed. Arica felt a moment of sympathy. Grandmother's full attention could be pretty intense.

"Connor, do you ever feel as though you don't quite belong where you are?" the Fairy Queen asked at last. "Do you ever wonder if you've lost something important, and think if you could just find it again, then everything would make more sense?"

"All the time," Connor admitted.

"What I'm trying to tell you," she concluded, "is that your father is one of those fairies who went to Earth to find the others. This means that you are half fairy, just like your cousin Arica, and you belong here just as much as the rest of us." She paused, then added, "Welcome home, Connor."

Connor just stared at her, with his mouth in a silly little O and his eyes blinking furiously.

"Look," the queen said, picking up the *Book of Fairies* and riffling through the pages. She held the book up to his nose and pointed. "Here is your father's name and here is yours right underneath it."

Connor squinted at the page for a few long moments. Then finally something seemed to click in his mind. He jumped to his feet. "Yes!" he cried, and leaped onto a chair. "Yes!" he yelled again. He hopped from the chair to the floor, then back to another chair, whooping and waving as he went. His third or fourth landing was a little off centre and the chair beneath him crashed to the floor with a terrible clatter, taking him along with it. Arica flinched and turned toward Grandmother, expecting to see the storm clouds gathering. Unbelievably, the old woman was laughing uncontrollably. Connor scrambled to his feet and pulled the chair upright, unhurt but somewhat subdued. But his joy was still so infectious that laughter started to bubble up through Arica's pain.

Later that night, as the two moons hung high in a velvet sky and the birds at her window finally fell silent, someone knocked on her bedroom door. She hadn't slept and didn't expect to for some time yet. Still, she was surprised to see her cousin wide awake and still dressed. He tiptoed in and perched on the edge of her bed. Moonlight from the window overhead fell in upon his glowing face and glinted off his two round lenses. With his bright eyes framed by thick glasses and his round head topped with all that tousled hair, what he most resembled was a wide-eyed, feather-headed owl.

"I've been thinking a lot about Aunt Lynn — I mean your mother — lately," he said.

Arica nodded, wondering why he was going to all this trouble to state the obvious. Wasn't that what everyone been doing?

"Your grandmother lent me the *Book of Fairies* to read," he continued eagerly, "As you know, it's full of spells, recipes, and lots of useful tips."

"Yes, I did know that," she said. She was beginning to see where all of this was leading and wondered why she hadn't thought of it herself.

"If the answer to your mother's problem is any-where, I'm guessing it will be in here." He shoved the book into her hands. "Since you can't sleep any-way, you might as well have something to do."

"Thanks, Connor," she said, touched by his thoughtfulness. She hugged the book against her chest and felt the magic of it tingle through her bones. If nothing else, that in itself would give her some comfort.

On his way out, he paused in the doorway and grinned back at her. "I'm sure things will all work out," he added, then closed the door behind him.

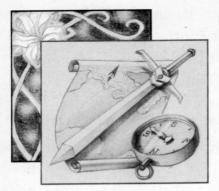

Chapter 7

The next morning Arica found her grandmother in the castle kitchen helping Doron do the breakfast dishes. She had never associated the Fairy Queen with such menial chores as pot scrubbing, but perhaps that was because she had never (until now) actually caught her in the act of doing it. At home there was always a dishwasher to take care of things.

"Grab a cloth," Grandmother said when Arica came bounding excitedly into the room. "With your help we'll be done in no time."

"No time" turned out to be much longer than she would have liked, but when the job was finally done, Grandmother joined her on a bench beside the cupboard. Doron glanced at them, hung up his towel, and politely exited the room.

"I've been studying the *Book of Fairies*," Arica explained, retrieving it from the table where she had set it, "and I found a recipe that might help Mother!" She spread the page open in front of Grandmother and read out loud:

CURE FOR ANY UNKNOWN POISON

*3 petals of a rainbow flower, found in the heart of
    a dragon's cave*
1 cup of clear spring water
A child's tear
2 hairs plucked from a unicorn's forelock
*Heat the water to boiling. Add the other ingredients.
Steep for 20 minutes. Strain the liquid; spoon into
the victim's mouth.*

Grandmother took the book from her hands and studied it for so long that Arica began to grow anxious. Surely she would agree that it was worth a try! Tracking down a rainbow flower might be a bit of a problem, but the rest of the ingredients could be found right here inside the Fairy Village. And as Grandmother herself had once said, the ancient knowledge that the *Book of Fairies* contained was written by the greatest and wisest of the fairies. So the way she saw it, if the recipe said it would cure any unknown poison, then it would do just that.

But Grandmother's eyebrows were hunched low over eyes that had suddenly lost their warmth. "The only place where you might find a rainbow flower is on Dragon Island," she stated, closing the book with a final-sounding thud. "I have a problem with you going there for any reason — "

"But — "

" — much less to look for a flower we don't really know exists," she continued.

"But it's right here in the *Book of Fairies*," Arica protested.

Grandmother shook her head. "The *Book of Fairies* is very old and contains a lot of information we don't understand," she explained. "Many of the recipes are real, some are myths, and some are only wishful thinking. I admit the book is filled with its own kind of magic, but that doesn't make it fool-proof."

"I have to go anyway," Arica insisted. "Even if there's only a small chance that I'll find the flower. I can't just give up. I'll take Connor and Wish with me. I've already talked to Connor — "

"You have no idea what you're up against," Grandmother said in a tone so frosty that it made Arica's skin prickle. An icy-voiced Grandmother was not good. Not good at all. But this was too important to let go without a fight, even thought Arica knew Grandmother didn't like to be argued with. She opened her mouth to explain some more, but Grandmother didn't give her the chance.

"Some people believe that dragons are as mythical as that rainbow flower," the queen continued, "but I know better. Dragons are few, but they are real. Your grandfather met one once. Of all fairies, he was the most powerful, and yet even he barely escaped with his life. They are more terrible and deadly than you can imagine. One look in a dragon's eye and you're paralyzed by magic, unable to even lift your arm against it. One blast from its breath and you're a puff of smoke and cinders on the wind."

"I don't care!" cried Arica. "I'd risk anything to make Mother well again!"

"Anything?" Grandmother's face was frightening, it was so cold and remote. "Your life? Your cousin's? Wish's? Unicorns and dragons are age-old enemies, Arica. No one knows why. And no one knows what would happen if two such enemies were to meet face to face."

Grandmother was silent then, lost in thought, frowning. She sighed at last. "I cannot keep you here against your will," she said, "but will you at least think it over for a while?"

Arica thought it over for three long days. She

paced up and down the castle hallways, hung out in the garden with Wish and sat beside her mother and waited for some sign of improvement in her condition. But the more she waited, and the more she thought about it, the more sure she became of what she had to do.

On the morning of the fourth day she asked Connor to meet her in the castle kitchen, where they set to work filling their backpacks with nuts, dried fruit, cheese, biscuits and even some Bundelag version of beef jerky. Arica had yet to see a cow in the place, so it was more likely sheep jerky or even goat jerky. She had eaten some before and it was actually quite tasty. Whatever the meat was, she stuffed lots of it into her bag. They were nearly finished packing when Doron came striding in to say that the Fairy Queen wanted to see them in the Great Hall.

When they entered the room, Grandmother rose from the table and turned toward them. She studied them for so long without speaking that Arica had to force herself not to fidget or break into nervous laughter. Beside her, Connor shifted from one foot to the other and whistled tunelessly under his breath. Arica couldn't remember ever seeing her grandmother look quite so careworn and weary.

"I have some things for you to take with you," the old woman said, much to Arica's surprise. Her voice was beyond cold, now. It was flat and dead. "Arica, here is your father's sword. You've used it before. I hope that its magic is strong enough to keep you alive until you're off the island. Connor, this sword belonged to your father when he was your age. Treat it with care and respect and it will serve you well. I'm also sending along a map of North Bundelag and a compass. I don't want to have to take time out of my busy schedule to come hunting for lost children." Her last words might have been bitter, but there was no bitterness in her voice, only a great sadness.

"Thank you, Grandmother," said Arica, feeling grateful and a little ashamed. She hadn't intended to add to her grandmother's already overwhelming burden.

The old woman made no reply, but continued to give instructions. "When you reach the farthest point on the north shore — directly north of Unicorn Valley — wait. I've sent word for one of my sailing ships to meet you there and carry you to Dragon Island. That way you won't have to waste time building a raft. My advice is to get on and off the island as quickly as possible. Do you have any questions?"

"No," said Connor with a squeak. He had never seen a person in such despair and didn't know quite how to respond. For that matter, neither did Arica.

"I'm sorry, Grandmother," she tried to explain,

"but I have to do this. You understand, don't you? Please, I need you to understand."

After a long pause, while each second that ticked by tore painfully at her heart, her grandmother nodded in acceptance. "I don't like it, but I understand," she said softly. "I would probably do the same." Then she gave Arica the kind of hug that told her she wouldn't rest easily — or maybe not at all — until they were safely home.

Wish caught up with them as they left the castle, and bounced playfully alongside as they made their way back to the meadow through the Fairy Village. At the end of the pathway Arica looked back just in time to see the Fairy Village blink out of sight, and in a twinkling, the bustling camp of elves reappeared in front of her. It seemed less crowded than before, and as they approached it an elf Arica had never met ran out to meet them. He threw a nervous glance at Wish, then began to speak. His words came in a garbled rush, as though the sounds had somehow become scrambled in their hurry to get out.

"Your friend Nue told me to tell you that he had to leave," the elf explained. "A group of human soldiers crossed the border between North and South Bundelag, and Nue took some men and went to help settle the skirmish."

"What about Perye and Drusa?" Arica asked, feeling a little sad that she had missed Nue.

The elf frowned. "They left this morning in a huge hurry. Their assignment was a secret one, but then Perye's assignments usually are. He does a lot of undercover work."

"Thanks, anyway," Arica said, and spoke over her shoulder to Connor. "Let's get started, then. I'm sure we'll see them when we get back."

They spent the next four days hiking across the open plains of North Bundelag in a northeasterly direction. They saw nothing and had no one for company except the birds that soared overhead, a few timid but curious deer, and some groundhogs that scurried beneath their feet. Insects buzzed around them in great abundance — especially the flies and mosquitoes. Arica doubted that there was a place in existence that didn't have some kind of fly or mosquito to bother the poor people who lived there. A world without them would simply be too good to be true. But she would take the insects any day over the pfipers, those poisonous little green snakes with wings that struck so viciously and without warning.

During the afternoon of the fourth day a whole new problem cropped up. Arica thought she sensed someone behind them, but when she turned her head, no one was there. Yet hour after hour the feeling persisted. By the time they stopped for the night she was beginning to jump and flinch at every bird twitter and rustle of the grass.

"What's wrong with you, anyway?" asked Connor after she had whirled around and stared out into the darkness for the third time in half an hour.

"Did you hear anything?" she whispered.

"Only the usual night noises," he replied, biting down on a chunk of roasted rabbit. Connor's hunting ability had improved immensely these past few days. Arica wished she could say the same for her cooking skills, but unfortunately, in spite of all her recent practice, she was still nearly hopeless at it. She had to admit that she sorely missed Nue's campfire stew.

You are right, True Arica, said Wish. *Something is out there, but I don't know who or what.*

Arica shivered and moved closer to the little fire that they had built out of clods of manure, dry grass, and a few small twigs. Travelling over the prairie had a couple of disadvantages over a journey through the forest — one, a lack of wood to burn, and two, fewer places to hide. "We'd better take turns keeping watch tonight," she suggested to Connor. "And maybe we should sleep on our swords. If there is something dangerous out there, we can't let it catch us by surprise."

"I agree," he mumbled through his meat.

In spite of Arica's fears the night passed without incident, and dawn found them once again travelling north and east. They had been walking for a little less than an hour when a sudden breeze from the north brought with it a gust of cool, damp air and the salty smell of the ocean. Arica paused in her tracks and breathed in deeply, then shouted with delight.

"We're almost there!" she cried. "Connor, can you smell it?"

"Of course I can," he said, grinning with anticipation. "I can hardly wait to go for a swim!"

But their joy was short-lived, for the next instant Wish whinnied in alarm. Arica whirled around, but saw nothing. The unicorn reared, her front hooves slashing at the air. Magic shimmered in the air near her, then gathered to one bright point a few metres from her nose. It didn't take Arica long to recognize the light for what it was. She had heard about this kind of spell from Perye, who prided himself on his vast knowledge of magic. It was called an invisibility spell, and only someone who was very adept at the art of casting spells could do it. The point of light grew stronger and then it burst open like the birthing of a tiny sun. Out from the centre stepped her uncle Raden, mounted on a tall, bay stallion.

Wish backed away from the man on the horse, prancing and snorting with anger. Connor drew his sword. It glittered in the morning sunlight. Her own sword was in the pack on her back. She let it slide to

Out from the centre stepped her uncle Raden, mounted on a tall, bay stallion.

the ground just in case she had to make a sudden grab for it.

"My goodness, you're a touchy bunch," came the deep, mocking voice. "Not that I blame you. You're a long way from home and you have no fairy queen to protect you."

"Cut out the chit-chat and get to the point," snapped Arica, not willing to put up with his usual mind games.

"Very well," he sneered. "If that's the way you want it, I'll explain. As I followed you for the past few days, I became more and more puzzled as to where you were going and what you were trying to do. Then it finally came to me. I heard a silly story once about a flower that grows in dragons' caves, and how it can cure every kind of poison. It's utter nonsense, of course, but it's just the kind of foolish tale you might believe. When I realized you were searching for the flower to heal your mother, I had the best laugh I've had in years!"

"If I'm so foolish," said Arica, "then why did you follow me? What have you got to worry about?"

Raden ignored her. "The way I see it," he continued, "whatever way this turns out, I win. If you come back empty-handed, I win. If a dragon devours you — by far the more likely event — I win again. And if, by some wild, improbable chance you do happen to find the flower and survive the dragon, I will find you before you even make it half a kilometre across the prairie."

"Why do you want to find me if you think the flower is a fake?" she asked.

"Because I don't like to take chances," he said.

Then he smiled that bitter, soulless smile that she knew so well, turned his back to them, and nudged his mount into a gallop. They watched him until he was only a small, black blemish upon a sea-green plain.

Chapter 8

Grandmother's sailing ship arrived just before noon. They waited on a beach of silver sand while the waves lapped in around their tired feet and gulls circled and shrieked above them. After a time a tiny, distant object appeared on the far horizon. They stood and watched as it drew nearer and nearer, making out first its huge white sails, then a hull of dark wood. At last it stopped and anchored just a few hundred metres off the shore. Some sailors lowered a rowboat into the water and two elves climbed in and started paddling toward the shore. When the elves were close enough to be recognized, Arica shouted with delight to see the familiar faces of Perye and his sister Drusa.

"So are we your secret assignment?" she asked when the greetings and hugs were done.

"Of course," replied Perye. "I volunteered for the job. Did you think I'd let you get away that easily?"

But when she looked at Drusa, all she saw were sad green eyes and a face shadowed with worry. "We're afraid for you, Arica," the elf girl said. "Have you really thought this through? Among our people there are stories told of dragons — terrible tales of long ago that are whispered late at night or in dark and hidden places — tales of elves maimed and scarred, of crops burned, and of animal bones heaped upon hillsides. Must you do this? Is there no other way?"

Arica shook her head. "Without the rainbow flower, my mother will probably never wake up. If it was your mother, what would you do?"

Drusa remained silent, for there was only one answer to that kind of question.

"Have any of your people ever seen a dragon?" asked Connor.

"No one that I know of," admitted Perye. "But that doesn't mean they don't exist."

"We'll come with you to the dragon's cave," offered Drusa. "With our help, you'll have a better chance."

"Thank you, but no," Arica replied. "I've had a lot

of time to think this over — a week, to be exact — and I know what will work best. We have to get in and out of the cave as quickly and quietly as possible, so the fewer people, the better. Where we need you the most is on the shore, waiting with the rowboat. Since we might be fleeing from a dragon, someone has to get us back to the sailboat in a big hurry — someone who isn't exhausted from the climb."

"That makes sense," admitted Perye.

Drusa frowned. "I still don't like it," she said. "It sounds dangerous."

"No matter how you put it," said Connor, "it's going to sound dangerous."

"The best thing to do, then, is get the job over with," said Perye practically. "Grab your things everyone, and throw them in the boat. Let's get out of here."

The words were hardly out of his mouth when a swarm of pfipers burst from the ground behind them.

Somewhere in the back of her mind Arica had sensed that during the past few minutes the beach had grown strangely quiet, but she had been so busy thinking about the task at hand that she had ignored her own inner warning. If only she had paid closer attention to the signs. The circling, cawing gulls had long since vanished from the sky, and even the tiny crabs that scurried endlessly across the sand had all disappeared into their holes.

Connor had never seen a pfiper before, so he was the slowest to react. While the rest were diving for the swords, he just stood and squinted through his glasses with his chin wagging and the pfipers' slithery green bodies whirling about his head. Arica had no time to worry about her cousin, but she figured he would snap out of his daze in a few seconds — as soon as the first pfiper sunk its centimetre-long fangs into his unprotected flesh.

Arica tore her sword from her pack and started swinging. In between thrusts she tried desperately to catch sight of Wish. Magic worked well against pfipers, and the battle would be over in an instant if she could only draw magic from the unicorn. But in order to do that, she needed Wish to be within a hundred-metre range — give or take a few metres. At the moment Wish was only a speck of white half a kilometre down the shore — too far away to be of any use. Why did she choose this particular time to go frolicking in the waves?

"Wish!" Arica shrieked as she stabbed. "Come back here! Hurry!"

Connor gripped his sword with both hands and hacked at the air, but this didn't keep the pfipers from bunching dangerously around him. A quick glance showed her that he had received some bites already.

Wish was tearing across the sand now, her mane and tail whipping out behind her like silver banners. Arica hoped, with intensity close to pain, that she would arrive in time to save them. Drusa fell to her knees, then struggled up again, her jaw clenched in grim determination. Perye howled with anger as he stabbed. Pfiper bodies littered the sand around them, glistened green and ghastly in the ocean froth, and writhed, bleeding, at their feet.

At last! Wish's magic was within range. Arica pulled the power from her horn and felt it rush through her arm and into her father's sword. She had no idea what would happen if she mixed the sword's magic with the unicorn's, but she had no time to worry about such minor details.

The sword in her hand glowed blue, then flared like a fire doused with gasoline. The blast of sound that followed was like a hammer in her brain, so she hardly noticed the sparks that spewed outward from the weapon's tip. The backlash struck her full in the chest, ripped the sword from her hand, and flipped her body through the air, end over end. She landed face down and rolled into the surf, only half-aware of what was happening. When she finally lifted her head and spit the sand from her teeth, she realized that the pfipers were gone and the attack was over.

So that was how it worked, she mused, as she pulled her battle-battered body upright. The magic of the sword mixed with the unicorn's magic produced a sudden release of power that was impossible to control. It was really quite astonishing, but not very practical if you needed to direct the burst of magic toward a target. Perhaps with some practice she could overcome the problem, though she doubted it.

"Oh, wow," said Connor. "That was a close one! When you told me about the flying snakes, I had no idea!"

Perye kicked one of the dead bodies with his toe and shuddered. "They're frightening all right, and quite deadly. Unfortunately, lots of elves die every year from pfiper bites. It's a problem we've never been able to solve. Let's get out of here before they come back."

"I'm with you," said Arica. She picked up her sword and slipped it back inside her pack. She should have known that such an easy, pleasant journey was too good to last.

She started to follow the others, but as she tiptoed her way through the scattered pfipers, she came to one that was still moving. It writhed and shuddered at her feet and made little peeping sounds, like a suffering baby bird.

She stopped and stood over it for a moment, her stomach churning with unease. Lying so helplessly in the sand as it was, it could be crushed easily beneath her heel. But for some reason Arica hesitated. It was one thing to destroy an enemy in the heat of battle to save your own life; it was quite another to kill a wounded, helpless creature who could hardly lift its head.

Besides, there was something very unusual about the wounded pfiper. For one thing, it was at least half again as long as the others, and it was the wrong colour. The common shade for pfipers was a pale, rather sickly green that reminded her of something a moose might clear from its nose. This one was a darker leaf green — and its skin was dotted with tiny flecks of blue that glittered like inlaid jewels.

She knelt down beside it and saw that its body was laid open to the bone in one huge gash. A pale eye stared up at her. She flinched with shock as that eye met hers, for this wasn't the look of a dull-eyed, dumb animal, driven by instinct alone. The look the creature gave her was intelligent and aware. But the most surprising part of it was that she saw neither anger nor hatred in that look — only an immense sadness.

"Perye," she called, rising to her feet again. "Come here."

Perye grumbled his way through the pfiper bodies until he stood beside her. He peered down. "Kill it," he said, and raised his foot.

"Wait a minute," Arica protested, pulling on his

arm. "There's something different about this one. You know a lot about pfipers. Let me ask you a question."

"All right, but make it quick. I want to get out of here."

"Who started the war?"

Perye stared at her as if she had just sprouted feathers and a beak. "What do you mean, who started the war? Pfipers are vicious killers. It's what they do! It's what they've always done!"

Arica shook her head. "I used to think that, too. Up until about ten seconds ago."

Connor clumped up beside them and gazed down at the pfiper with intense interest. It was bleeding less rapidly now, as though it were running out of blood. It gave a sudden shudder, then went limp.

"Poor thing," Connor murmured.

Perye rolled his eyes towards the sky. "Are you both crazy?" he hooted. "Five minutes ago this overgrown worm was having you for lunch. If it could, it would do the same again!"

Drusa joined them beside the pfiper. "I don't know what you're all so worked up about," she said reasonably. "It looks like it will be dead soon, anyway."

Arica backed up to make room for Wish as she nudged her way into their little circle. She lowered her head and sniffed at the pfiper, then looked up at

Arica in a puzzled way, as though she didn't quite understand what all the fuss was about.

"I have a theory," Arica announced. "Maybe a long time ago their ancestors and yours got off to a bad start, and because of that misunderstanding, they're still fighting — because they think they have to. That's logical, don't you think? They don't eat us, so why do they attack?"

"For the sheer joy of it," said Perye, turning away in disgust.

"Another theory — I think pfipers are like the bees we have at home. I believe this is their queen. Look at how much bigger and how unusual she is. Maybe we invaded their hive, or at least the area where their hive is, and they're just protecting themselves."

"That sounds more likely to me," said Drusa. "The first theory's an interesting one, though." Her curiosity satisfied, she turned away and followed her brother back toward the boat.

Arica rubbed her hand over Wish's neck. "You're going to think I'm crazy," she said, smoothing a tangle from the unicorn's mane, "but will you do something for me?"

You know I will, True Arica.

Arica gestured at the nearly dead animal on the ground. "Will you please heal the pfiper with your horn?" she asked. "I can't just walk away and leave the poor creature bleeding in the sand. It doesn't seem right, somehow."

Of course, said Wish.

Arica and Connor stepped back to give the unicorn more room. At Arica's command Wish lowered her horn, and when its golden tip touched the pfiper's ravaged body, it began to glow with a soft blue light. Then, right before their astonished eyes (for this aspect of unicorn magic never ceased to astonish even Arica), the ragged edges of the wound closed and sealed. When the light finally faded, the pfiper's skin was smooth and scar-free and, except for a tiny red spot where Wish's horn had made contact, it was as well and whole as ever.

Arica pulled Wish back, uncertain about what the pfiper might do next. On finding itself healed, would it attack again? She thought not, but one could never be too sure. It remained on the ground for a moment longer and stared up at them through pale, lidless eyes. Its body trembled and its wings hummed. It shook its head, as if confused, then seemed to arrive at a decision. It shot straight up into the air, made a large, buzzing loop around their heads, and darted away.

"I'm glad that's over!" exclaimed Connor. He grinned at her and rubbed his palms together in a series of rapid swishes. "We're out of here! Nothing can stop us now!"

. . . it began to glow with a soft blue light.

Later, Arica was to remember that statement and wonder how her cousin could have been so wrong. But the poor boy had had no idea about how pfiper venom worked on its victim's body.

She was the last one to the rowboat, and as she paused beside it for one last look back at North Bundelag, she gasped in surprise. A group of unicorns was galloping toward them, and although they were no more than a few moving spots on the horizon, she sensed their presence as strongly as if they were standing right beside her. Wish felt them too, and raised her head. She whinnied joyfully at the same moment as Arica felt the gentle, tingling touch of their thoughts upon her mind.

True One, they said.

"Light?" she cried with delight. It had been so long since she had seen Light, the magnificent stallion that was Wish's father. He was the first unicorn she had met on her first journey to Bundelag.

True One, said Light again. His thoughts came to her, clear and warm with affection, and the urgency behind them prickled in her mind like pain. *Don't take my foal to the place where the dragons live,* she heard the stallion plead. *If you do, it could be the end of all unicorns.*

Chapter 9

There were five unicorns in all — Light, his mate Song, and three others that Arica had never seen before. As they thudded to a halt just metres from where she stood beside her friends, the sight of so much grace and beauty all in one place nearly took her breath away. She had to fight the urge to rush into their midst, throw her arms around each one of their necks in turn, and kiss their velvet noses.

She shook her head to clear it, and wondered why she was suddenly so overcome with emotion. It was true that she loved all of the unicorns, but her father often said she was tough as nails, so why was she reacting this strongly? Perhaps she was just gladder than usual to see them. Unfortunately, they didn't seem quite as happy to see her. It was clear by the way their dark, gentle eyes were fixed so sadly upon her that something was seriously wrong.

Perye and Drusa watched from the boat. This didn't surprise her, for the reverence most elves had for unicorns bordered on fear, and her elf friends probably didn't want to offend the honoured animals. Connor's attitude was more practical. Although he admired and respected the unicorns, he had no long history with them, and his experience with the horses on his father's ranch gave him confidence.

"What do you mean 'the end of all unicorns'?" Arica asked Light.

"Is someone going to destroy the unicorns?" squawked Connor, who had only heard her side of the conversation. "If it's true, we have to protect them!"

"You're jumping to conclusions," she said. "I'll tell you all about it when I know more."

Light tossed his head and pranced restlessly back and forth in front of her. His nostrils flared as he breathed, and his mane tumbled over his neck like splashing water.

Listen to me, True One, he said, *for I have an important story to tell. A long time ago, before humans came to Bundelag, dragons lived among us. They were* proud and selfish beasts. They ruled the sky above and hunted the earth below. They took what they wanted, when they wanted it, for no one had the strength to withstand them. No one, that is, except our kind. For although the dragons' magic was dark and powerful, and their fire hotter than melting stone, our magic could withstand them. And only our horns could pierce their scales to the tender flesh beneath.*

From there, Song took up the tale. *Elves, fairies, trolls and ogres — all came to us for help. And we agreed that the pillage and slaughter had to stop. The war that followed was slow and quiet, but as brutal as your wars. Every time one of us caught a dragon in the act of stealing or killing there was a fight to the death. We were equally matched foes. After years of duels, we realized that both dragons and unicorns would soon become extinct.*

We called for truce, and met with the dragons, continued Light. *Seven of us and four of them were all that was left in all of Bundelag. After many days, both sides made a pledge. We pledged that no unicorn would ever again use its magic against a dragon. They pledged that they would never again plunder or steal, and would kill only what they needed for food. Then they withdrew to the large island in the north, and we to the Unicorn Valley opposite that island. To this day, we have both kept our part of the bargain.*

Arica was silent, digesting this for a while. Finally,

she understood. "You're afraid that if Wish comes with me," she said slowly, "she'll use her magic against the dragon to protect me."

Yes, said Light. *If she sees that you are in danger, she will defend you in the best way she knows. And as soon as she uses her magic, the truce will end, and the dragons will rise up against all in Bundelag.*

Arica turned back to Connor and the elves. She wasn't sure if she could make it through the whole awful story without her stomach twisting up inside of her like cold spaghetti, but somehow she managed. When she was done they just stood there, too stunned to speak. The silence seemed to last forever — a silence thick with sorrow for Arica's mother, for themselves, and especially for the unicorns. Before them the sunlight dazzled like diamonds on the blue-green sea, but it was hard for Arica to enjoy the splendour when inside she felt as though she might die of grief.

Don't go, True One, pleaded Song. *We need you. All of Bundelag needs you. Without Wish's magic to protect you, the risk is too great. Our ancient enemies are very powerful.*

"I have to try," she said, wanting them to somehow understand. "My mother needs me."

Beside her Wish nickered, and she felt the warm tickle of the animal's breath against her neck. She reached out in gratitude for the comfort that was being offered, but Wish had already turned back toward her parents.

Father, Mother, the little unicorn said. *There is a way I can go with True Arica and still not break the pledge.*

Light and Song stiffened. Their nostrils flared in alarm.

"What do you mean, Wish?" Arica asked, knowing, by the stab of anguish coming from the minds of Light and Song, that it couldn't be anything good.

Light pranced around the litter of pfiper bodies and back again as he fought to calm himself. He snorted and pawed at the sand with his hoof. *My foal is referring to something that is dangerous and rarely done,* he said. *She wants us to take away her magic.*

It felt like a blow to her gut. "How?" Arica managed to gasp out. "I don't understand."

It can't be done unless a unicorn is willing, Light explained. His words pinged in her brain like snapping strings. *If Wish desires it, we can pull her magic into ourselves, the way you take her magic for your own use. When you do it, you use only a portion. We would take it all, and so it is dangerous. Without her magic, she cannot live long. Without her magic, she will die.*

"But — but — that's absurd!" stammered Arica. She turned to Wish. "What are you thinking? Without your magic you'll have no protection against the dragon!"

But neither will you, True Arica, Wish pointed out. *And you need my speed to stay ahead of the dragon and carry you down the mountain. Fairies are powerful and wise in many ways, but not swift on their feet.*

It was the easiest decision Arica had ever made. "No, Wish," she said. "Thank you for the brave and generous offer, but I can't let you do this. Please stay here with your parents, and I'll see you when I return from Dragon Island."

She paid no attention to the flood of protest that welled up inside of Wish's mind, but instead, gave the unicorn a final hug goodbye.

"Thank you," she said to the others. "I'll see you soon."

We'll be waiting, Light replied.

True One? said Song as she turned to go.

Arica stopped and looked back. "What is it, Song?" she asked.

I can still help you in one way, by saving you days of searching. When you reach the island, travel along the part of the shore that faces the rising sun. You'll come to a mountain that grows up out of the sea. One of the dragons lives there.

"Thank you, Song," she said.

Be careful, True One. We need you.

"What was that all about?" Connor asked as she scrambled into the boat. The unicorns remained where they were and silently watched. She kept her back to them so she wouldn't have to see their large, sad eyes as they followed her, but she could still feel them.

"Wish wants to come with us," she informed her cousin. "She wants the other unicorns to take away her magic. I won't allow it, of course."

The look Connor gave her was almost a scowl. "I don't think you have the right to make that kind of decision," he said. "After all, you're risking your life for your mother, even though your Grandmother didn't want you to. Yet you won't let Wish risk her life for you."

"I don't want to talk about it," she said, and plopped down in the rowboat. She leaned back and closed her eyes, hoping that he would take the hint and leave her alone in her misery. Fortunately he did, for he just shrugged his shoulders and turned away. The next time she looked, they were halfway to the sailing ship and the unicorns had disappeared.

Their group was welcomed on board the larger boat by an elf that reminded Arica somewhat of Nue in that he was built short and round, and had hair like an overgrown prickle bush. Perye introduced him as the captain, which explained why he was in such a hurry. He nodded briskly, gave each of their hands a quick pump, then rushed away.

Arica didn't know anything about sailing — in

fact the whole idea of going so far away from land
without a motor for backup made her more than a
little uneasy — but even she was impressed by what
she saw. Elves scurried like ants across the deck, pul-
leys rattled and squealed, and the boards beneath
her feet creaked as if with excitement.

"Come with me," said Drusa, taking her arm. "I'll
show you to my room. We're the only girls on board,
so you'll bunk with me. You look like you could use
a rest. That was a terrible disappointment with the
unicorns, but remember that we're all still behind
you."

Arica nodded gratefully. She drank the juice

. . . they were halfway to the sailing ship and the unicorns had disappeared.

Drusa pushed into her hands, lay down on a small hard bunk in a room the size of her parents' closet, and closed her eyes. Sometime during the past half-hour she had developed a stabbing headache. At the moment her life felt like a stack of collapsing cards, and she had no idea which one might topple next.

She must have dozed off, for the next thing she knew a loud thump jarred her awake. Something was delaying the boat's departure. Excited shouts filled her ears. A flurry of thudding boots stampeded over her head. After a minute or two of some similar non-sense, she gave up and rolled off the bed. She arrived on the deck just in time to see the elves sling a large, pale animal up over the side of the boat and dump it ungracefully onto the deck.

At first she thought it was a shark or even a small whale, but when she pushed her way through the clump of sailors that surrounded it, she saw four hooves and a long, sodden tail. A moment later it raised its poor, bedraggled head and she realized that the elves had snagged themselves a horse, though she had no idea what it had been doing so far out to sea.

"The poor thing is half drowned," said one of the sailors.

A clump of seaweed was caught in the horse's mane and wound around its ears like a knot of tangled snakes. Water dribbled from its hide and puddled on the deck beneath its body, and when it coughed, more sprayed from its throat. As she stepped nearer, it raised its head and whinnied plaintively. She stared back at it and her knees suddenly turned to mush. If Connor hadn't grabbed her by the arm she would have collapsed flat onto the deck.

She knew the animal now. This was no ordinary horse that the sailors had fished up from the sea's salty depths. This was her own beloved Wish — weak and dull, now that her magic and her horn were gone.

Arica tried to speak, but nothing came from between her lips but a small, deep-throated gurgle.

She wiped her hand across her face in one rapid, angry swipe.

Don't cry, True Arica, the unicorn said. *You have to help your mother — nothing can stop you. So it is for me. I have to help you. Nothing can stop me.*

Chapter 10

Sometime during the night the pfiper poison finally caught up with them.

Arica woke up first, with a headache and an unpleasant churning in her stomach. She lay in her bed for a time and willed it to go away, without much success. Beside her, Drusa shivered and groaned in pain. A while later she heard the sound of frantic running feet, followed by someone being sick over the side of the boat.

She staggered on deck to a cold, windless night and a ship stalled helplessly upon a sea of black glass. His distasteful task completed, Connor had stumbled over to a barrel and was collapsed weakly against it. He squinted at her in an attempt to figure out who she was. The light of two moons shone down on her cousin's faintly greenish skin and made bruises of the hollows beneath his eyes. Obviously his glasses had been left behind in the rush.

"Are you all right?" she asked, collapsing on the deck beside him.

"Oh, it's you," he said. "That's an extremely dumb question. As anyone can tell just by looking, I'm not all right at all." He paused, then added: "You don't look too great yourself."

Something that looked hazy and pale in the moonlight drifted around a corner and stopped next to them. Connor reached up to fondle an inquiring nose, then groaned, pushed the animal away, and dashed back across the deck. Arica tried her hardest not to listen, but from what she did hear, it sounded as though there was a lot of work going on without much result. The boy's stomach was obviously empty.

If I had my magic, I could heal you, said Wish with a touch of regret.

"It's all right," Arica assured her. "We haven't got it very bad. If we did, we wouldn't be able to run around like this. We would be flat on our backs in bed. I figure we'll all be as good as new by morning."

I hope you're right, True Arica.

"Don't worry," she said. "Around here, I'm the

expert on pfiper poison." A sudden thought struck her. "Why can you and I still talk? I thought we needed your magic for that."

It's your magic that makes the talking happen, not mine, Wish replied. *It's a gift you have that makes you different from everyone else in Bundelag.*

She was about to question Wish further when Connor clumped back and flopped down beside her. He shivered, and his teeth clacked in his head like tiny hammers. Arica felt his forehead — that's what her mother did when she was sick. It felt cold and clammy.

"You should go back to bed," she advised. "You'll feel better if you keep warm." He nodded and heaved himself up, groaning. By the time she had followed him all the way down to his bed and settled him in beside Perye, who was also groaning, Arica was so wide awake it seemed like hours before she finally got to sleep again. The good thing about it was, the fresh air had eased her headache and settled her stomach.

By morning the wind had picked up again and was pushing tatters of grey cloud across a sunless sky. Arica took one look around, shivered, and rushed back inside to dig her jacket from the bottom of her pack. True to her prediction, Connor was up and about, none the worse for his experience except for a slight pallor to his cheeks.

The ship sailed briskly over a sea of gentle swells,

and by late morning Dragon Island loomed large and dark on the distant horizon. As they drew near, Arica could make out a scattering of purple mountains rising bleakly above the darkness of the trees.

"It looks like an ordinary island to me," said Perye, "and I don't see any dragons."

They skimmed closer. A rock-strewn beach spread out before them, then sloped up gradually to join with the forest's edge. This was certainly no tropical island. The trees were all pine and spruce, thin and scraggly, and packed tightly together as if searching futilely for warmth. Strangely, she saw no fish leaping in the water around them, and no gulls circling above the empty beach.

"It seems awfully quiet around here," said Drusa. "I'm getting a bad feeling."

Following the directions Arica had received from Song, their captain ordered the elves to adjust the sails, and their boat veered toward the east. "It can't be too long, now," Connor said. As it turned out, he was right. Sometime around two in the afternoon by Arica's estimation, they arrived at the place that Song had told them about.

The mountain lay just off the eastern coast and was separated from the main island by a narrow strip of water. On its lower slope, it managed to sustain a few thinly scattered trees and the occasional patch of shrubs and weeds. Above that, its bleak, bare torso thrust upward hundreds of metres, marked by deep fissures, jagged edges, and ridges that ended in the middle of nowhere.

At Arica's request, they continued northward and rounded the mountain, until they saw that the more hospitable back side sloped gradually up from a shore of sand and stone. With relief she saw that it looked almost possible to climb.

The captain anchored the ship as close to the island as he could get and instructed the elves to lower the rowboat. The only items Arica and Connor planned to take with them were enough food for one meal, some water, the flashlight and their swords, for the lighter they travelled, the more quickly they could move.

Fifteen minutes later they stood at the base of the mountain ready to begin their climb. Drusa and Perye would remain with the rowboat to wait for their return.

After numerous hugs and good luck wishes from the elves, they began their long journey up the mountain. It was slow and gruelling work, and by the time they reached the top some hours later, every muscle in Arica's body throbbed with complaint and every drop of water had been drained.

They sat on a stretch of bare rock facing a great ridge and nibbled half-heartedly on their biscuits and jerky. Judging by Connor's lack of appetite, she concluded his stomach must feel as queasy as hers did. There wasn't a weed or a blade of grass in sight, so Wish just stood quietly nearby and rested.

From her place on the rock, Arica could see three caves and something that might possibly be a fourth. The nearest cave opening was the size of a small house and revealed an interior blacker than a bear's den. The others looked even larger and every bit as foreboding. A chilly wind whistled past her ears and blew its way beneath her jacket. She shivered and folded her arms against her chest for warmth.

"Are you ready?" Connor whispered when they were done resting.

She just nodded, not wanting to alert any sleeping dragons. Rising to her feet, she led the way toward the first cave. A blast of cold air avalanched over them as they stepped inside. Her flashlight's beam cut a slice through the darkness and expanded outwards into a pale oval of light. Beside her, Wish's hooves clattered out a rhythm on the cold stone floor and echoed hollowly from the vaulted ceiling. It took them only a few moments to determine that the cave held neither flowers nor dragons, so they exited quickly and moved on to the next.

The second cave was noticeably warmer, though it had an odd smell that Arica couldn't quite place. Thankfully, she saw no dragon. To the right of them loomed a huge mound of reddish rock, and to the

. . . a pathway that wound around a rubble of boulders . . .

left a pathway that wound around a rubble of boulders and opened into a huge, dimly lit cavern.

The source of the light was a crack in the ceiling through which a small amount of sunlight had managed to trickle. But as they rounded the boulders, this wasn't what amazed her most.

One corner of the cavern was ablaze with flowers of every colour imaginable. As she watched, one flower turned from red to orange and then to yellow, while the one beside it started out green, darkened to blue and then ended with violet. Such rapid change, such mad explosions of colour, should have given her a headache. But rather than being a strain on the eyes and nerves, the effect was actually soothing.

"Oh, wow," said Connor. "Those have *got* to be rainbow flowers."

Something here feels strange to me, True Arica, said Wish.

"I can feel it, too," she replied with awe. "It must be the flowers."

She stepped up to the nearest patch of them and sank to her knees. There was something almost holy about these exquisite flowers growing in the barren heart of this cold and silent cave. She sensed their magic deep within her bones. If they couldn't save her mother, then nothing could.

She reached out with her hand to pluck three

petals from the nearest plant. That was all she need-ed — she would take no more than that.

The flower slipped through her fingers like running water and her hand came up empty.

She tried again, then again and again. To her dismay she realized that the plant wasn't about to let itself be picked, at least not by her.

Then Connor tried, but with no more success. Wish's attempt failed as well, though her lips closed over the petals with great care.

Arica remained where she was, too stunned with disappointment to move. The stones beneath her bruised her knees and made her ankles ache, but she hardly noticed. She just crouched there with her hands over her face, breathing slowly in and out, and told herself over and over not to panic. There had to be a way, if only she could think of what it was.

After a brief silence, Connor cleared his throat. "One time my mom had ants in her kitchen," he said. "They were crawling all over the countertops."

Arica raised her head. "What do ants on counter-tops have to do with anything?" she asked, only half listening. She had to think harder.

"They were getting into the food," he said.

"And?" Perhaps she could find a stick and dig one of the flowers up by its roots. No, that wouldn't work. They were growing right out of solid rock.

She reached out with her hand to pluck three petals . . .

"My mother tried everything, but nothing worked. Finally, I talked to the ants and asked them to leave."

She was starting to follow Connor's line of reasoning. He wanted her to talk to the flowers. It was the most ridiculous idea she had ever heard.

"The next day they were gone, and they never came back. What I'm trying to say is, maybe you should explain your problem to the flowers and ask them for help."

Maybe his idea wasn't so ridiculous after all. If one thing was clear, it was that the flowers couldn't be forced.

Do as Connor suggests, said Wish. *What do you have to lose?*

The flowers shimmered before her like a group of friendly children. As she pondered, she found herself smiling. Yes, what did she have to lose? She felt no malice from them, only gentleness and acceptance. She held out her hand toward them in a gesture of greeting, tried not to think about how silly she felt, and spoke.

"I'm Arica," she said. "This is my cousin Connor, and that's my friend Wish. We have come a long way to find you because we need your help. My mother is very ill, and you're the only ones who can save her. If it's possible — if it's not asking too much — could you please give us three small petals? We would be extremely grateful." She paused, wondering what else to say, then added, "Please help me."

The flowers continued to flicker happily, but nothing else. She sighed and rose to her feet. She rubbed her hand across her stinging eyes. "I don't know what to do anymore," she groaned. "I'm open to suggestions."

"Look," said Connor.

Three petals floated up from the midst of the flowerbed, fluttered through the air like tiny bodiless wings and hovered above her, as if waiting. "Oh," she said, and reached out again. An instant later they settled on her outstretched hand. She stared down at them in amazement and delight, hardly daring to believe her eyes.

"Thank you," she managed to whisper through a throat suddenly paralyzed with gratitude. "Thank you so much."

She slipped the petals carefully into the pocket of her jeans and hesitated, wondering if she dared to stay a moment longer and enjoy the beauty of the flowers. But suddenly Wish's nose butted against her, shoving her forward.

Hurry! the unicorn cried. *I know what's wrong with this place, now. The dragon has been here all along! It disguised itself with magic!*

Dragon? Here all along? Disguised with magic? Arica stared frantically around. Something had changed all right, but she wasn't exactly sure what. The path they had followed was still in the same place. The litter of small boulders hadn't moved. The cave entrance lay directly behind them, just as it should. Where was the dragon, then?

One more look and she had it. The huge mound of red rock she had noticed upon entering the cave had shifted.

She blinked. Not only had it shifted, it had also suddenly sprouted two huge golden eyes, some rows of wicked, yellow teeth and an enormous barbed tail.

Chapter 11

It was clear to Arica that they had grossly underestimated the size and strength of their foe.

Don't look into its eyes, Wish warned. *You'll get caught in the magic.*

She hadn't thought the beast would be so lizard-like or so quick. Something the size of a bulldozer had no right to move that fast. Its huge, horned head whipped around as they took off running, revealing teeth like sharpened stakes. It slithered after them, its dagger claws scraping over the rough stone floor. Its blood-red body bristled with scales, and a tail like a felled tree writhed behind it as it crawled.

Connor plunged through the cave doorway just

ahead of her. A quick glance around showed her how truly desperate their situation was, for there wasn't a boulder or a tree in sight, and she was certain they'd never outrun the beast.

Behind them, she heard Wish whinny in alarm, but even as she hesitated, she sensed that the unicorn's fear was for her and Connor more than for herself. Sure enough, Wish burst from the cave with a roaring, thundering dragon on her tail. As its massive body cleared the cave entrance, it paused for an instant as if deciding what to do next. Then it lunged after Arica.

She wondered, as the giant beast bore down upon her, why it didn't simply blast her into cinders with its heat and save itself all this trouble. Perhaps it needed a bit more time to stoke the fire. Its head descended. She smelled the hot, metallic odour of its breath as its jaws closed in upon her.

All she could do was hope that her death would be quick and painless, though she had doubts about the painless part. In a final attempt to save herself, she dropped to the ground, hoping this would give her a few seconds more of precious life. She had no idea what she might do with those few seconds, but at the moment that seemed unimportant. Above her, she heard the dragon bellow in rage, and opened her eyes just in time to see it fling its mighty head backward.

Wish's teeth were clamped tightly down upon the tip of its huge, snaky tail.

Arica leaped to her feet and drew her sword from her belt. At the same instant as the deadly tail flung Wish aside like a sack of rags, she stabbed upward with all her strength, plunging the end of her father's sword into the dragon's breast.

It was like poking an elephant with a pin. Her sword bounced back, tossing her roughly to the ground. Out of the corner of her eye she saw Connor hack wildly at its leg with his own weapon, but the creature paid him no more attention than a mammoth would to a mouse nipping at its feet.

Wish struggled up onto all four legs and stumbled back toward them. The dragon's breast swelled. Air hissed into its lungs, followed by a rumbling that came from deep within its throat. Then a ball of orange flame exploded from between its jaws and hurtled toward the unicorn.

"Wish!" Arica screamed, but already it was too late. Wish saw the approaching blast and flung herself aside, but not quickly enough. The edge of the fire caught the back of her neck as it streaked past, and the next instant her mane was red with flames.

Without stopping to think, Arica dashed forward. She saw with relief that although Wish was clearly terrified, she still had enough sense to roll on the ground in an attempt to douse the fire. Arica scrambled

Then a ball of orange flame exploded from between its jaws . . .

toward her, tore off her jacket, and threw it over the unicorn's neck. A moment later Connor rushed up with his sweater in his hand and joined her in trying to smother the flames.

Thankfully the fire was soon out, but a sudden rush of wind told her that the dragon had taken to the air and was hovering not more than half a dozen metres above them. Its great, dark body seemed to fill the entire sky. It stared down for a long moment out of those glittery golden eyes, pinning her where she stood. Beside her, Connor blinked and froze, caught in the same terrible spell. Wish lay silently on the ground, no longer moving, her once-beautiful mane a row of charred, black bristles.

Air hissed into the dragon's lungs. Its throat rumbled. Its wings beat. This was it, then. In a moment they would be three heaps of cinders upon the mountainside, just as Grandmother had said.

The dragon roared and the rocks rattled beneath their feet. Fire spewed forth — but, unbelievably, the deadly ball arced high into the air above their heads, like a rising sun. And at the same instant that Arica saw the sphere of heat shoot up, she saw what it was directed at. Closing in on the dragon was the most enormous swarm of pfipers she had ever seen.

The dragon's hold on them fell away like a sloughed skin. Wish scrambled to her feet, and Arica could see that one side of her ribcage was scraped raw from her tumble over the ground.

Now the dragon was entirely surrounded by pfipers. They circled its great head, nipped at its nose and eyes, and dived beneath its belly. The dragon bellowed and snapped, dashed its head and flung its mighty tail, but still the pfipers came. Arica shook her head in confusion. What were the pfipers doing way up on this mountain anyway, and why were they attacking the dragon and leaving the three of them alone?

As if in answer to her silent question, a single pfiper glided toward her, then paused and fluttered just metres away. It was a pfiper slightly larger than the others, with a skin of forest green flecked with dots as blue and bright as sapphires. The eyes that gazed into hers were clear and intelligent, and the look in them told her that now it was saving her life in thanks for saving its own.

She stared back, too surprised to speak. The pfiper hovered in the air a moment longer as if telling them to hurry and go, then darted away to join the fight.

"Wish!" she cried when her voice could make sound again. "Can you still run?"

I can, True Arica.

"Connor?"

"I'm fine," her cousin said.

"Then let's get out of here," she said. "I don't know how long pfipers can hold off the dragon."

The trip down the mountain was a nightmare of anxiety and pain, for they had no choice but to ride the wounded unicorn, and just as Arica had once felt the agony of Light's wounds, she was now experiencing Wish's. And her own, for she knew that she herself was to blame.

Don't punish yourself, True Arica, Wish said as she ran. *It's what I came for. I promised I would protect you and carry you safely down the mountain.*

But this didn't make Arica feel any better.

It seemed like an eternity before they finally reached the bottom and the place where Perye and Drusa waited so patiently for their return. The elves saw them coming and dashed forward, lifting them off Wish's tired back. Perye's lips tightened when he saw the unicorn's burns and scrapes and Drusa's eyes grew wide with alarm, but neither of them spoke. "Hurry," was all Arica said as they climbed into the boat. "Hurry!"

Later that night, with the island and the dragon farther and farther behind them, and with Wish's wounds cleaned and swabbed with a healing ointment provided by the elves, Arica told them the story of their miraculous escape. When she was done, Drusa laughed with joy and hugged them all, but Perye shrugged and turned away. Just before dawn the next morning, Arica found him standing all alone on the deck gazing out to sea while the light from two moons made emeralds of his eyes and turned his hair to gold.

"Are you angry with me?" she asked, stepping near to him.

He shook his head and, after a long moment of silence, he replied. "I hate to admit when I'm wrong, and I hate being wrong even more, but I have to say that I was wrong about the pfipers. I've spent a long, sleepless night thinking it over."

Arica giggled. "You just need to be wrong more often," she said. "That way, you'd be totally used to it — like I am." He joined her in laughter, and when they were done, his arm slipped quietly about her shoulders.

"I should have known a dragon could never get the best of you," was all he said.

The following day they anchored the ship beside the north shore of Bundelag, and Wish rejoined her joyful parents, who were anxious to restore her magic immediately. But it would take at least a week, they told Arica, for Wish to fully rest and heal.

As Arica stroked Wish's noble, hornless brow in a gesture of farewell, she remembered that she still needed two hairs from a unicorn's forelock, and Wish's had been burned away by one terrible blast of the dragon's breath. Song must have read her thoughts, for she immediately stepped forward and lowered her head.

Take mine, True One, she said. *I would be honoured to help.*

The unicorns' final gift was a warning: Raden, they said, was waiting for her nearby. Gladly, Arica accepted the captain's offer of further passage back to the Fairy Village. Going by ship was a safer and more logical way, especially now that they didn't have Wish to carry them.

They set sail immediately, expecting to arrive at the Fairy Village within three days. For Arica, it was a time of relaxing in the sun, of eating and sleeping, of telling stories, and of getting to know her cousin and her elf friends a little better, under less trying circumstances. The time passed in a pleasant haze of laughter, games, and engaging conversation, so the unexpected way that their journey ended came as an even greater shock.

On the afternoon of the third day, as they approached the shore where the Fairy Village was located, the captain sought them out as Arica and Connor battled over a game of cards.

"There's a ship following us," he told them without preamble. "I think you should take a look."

It was a ship all right, though not one of the more attractive ones she'd seen. Dirty sails reared above a dark, squalid hull. A white painted skull leered at them from its bow. Small dark men, too distant to be seen clearly, scuttled like beetles across its deck and then disappeared, as if trying to hide.

"That's a troll ship," said the captain tersely.

Something slimy crawled over Arica's skin.

"Raden!" she said.

Chapter 12

Hastily, they put together a plan. Connor and the others would stay and fight off Raden and the trolls, while Arica took the boat and rowed speedily for shore. Once there, she would flee to the Fairy Village and the Fairy Queen's protection. Arica didn't like the idea of taking off and leaving the others to fight her battle, but what choice did she have? If Raden got his hands on the petals, then their entire journey — including Wish's selfless courage — would have been for nothing.

The sailors steered toward the shore, then halted as near to it as they could get without running their ship into the ground. By that time the trolls' boat was so close that Arica could see every wart and wrinkle on their filthy skins, and a whiff of salty air brought with it the stink of their unwashed bodies. She had never met a troll yet that smelled anything but awful, and wondered how Raden, being as short on patience as he was, managed to put up with it.

There was no time for goodbyes as she swung down into the waiting rowboat and pushed away from the larger ship. Connor hung down over the railing and mouthed the words "Good luck." An instant later he was gone. Behind him the trolls were already boarding, and the shouts and clangs of sword against sword pushed her to row even harder.

The shore, which had seemed so close from the ship, she now realized was a good half-kilometre away. She rowed until the muscles in her arms burned with fatigue, forcing herself to focus on getting to land and not on what was happening back at the ship. At last her rowboat struck sand. She flung the oars down and leaped into the water — shoes, socks and all. Plunging through the knee-deep waves, she arrived at a wide, golden beach that stretched out as far as she could see in both directions.

Arica had never come at the Fairy Village from the sea side before. How was she to find it, before Raden found her? She would have to trust in the expertise of her grandmother's sailors, who had promised to drop her as close to the village as they could get. With that in mind, she headed straight inland at a dead run.

She had only gone a hundred metres when she noticed something small and dark coming along the beach toward her. It didn't take her long to discern that the object was a man on a horse. A short minute later she recognized both the man and the horse. The trolls and their ship had been a decoy, then. She should have realized that her escape from Grandmother's ship had been too easy. Raden had wanted her to come to shore by herself and she had fallen right into his trap.

There was no hope of outrunning him, of course. She stared wildly around, seeking a way of escape. Behind her lay the ocean and her abandoned row-boat. If she dashed back, with luck she might make it far enough out into the water that he couldn't follow. No — horses were good swimmers. In front of her was a grassy slope that led upwards to a meadow, hopefully the one where the Fairy Village and the camp of elves were located. If she could just get to the top, she would bellow for help as loudly as she could . . .

Her decision made, she plunged up the slope.

Raden caught up with her in less than a minute and leaped from his mount before its legs had even slowed. His eyes burned with a dark satisfaction and his black cloak billowed around him as he closed in upon her. The sword in his hand caught the sunlight and tossed it in her eyes. She raised one hand to block the glare, then with the other, pulled her own sword from her belt. He must realize that she wouldn't just hand the petals over without a fight. This was her mother's life she carried in her pocket. Her uncle smirked as he stopped directly in front of her, and their two swords struck.

In Arica's world swordplay was only a sport, and certainly not one intended for children. It went without saying that she had never learned the correct moves. But that's where the magic of her father's sword took over. It met Raden's weapon blow for blow, and everywhere she needed it to be, it was. But even as she stabbed and parried, she could feel herself being slowly driven back by his greater strength and skill, and she knew it was only a matter of time before he overcame her. He knew it too, and laughed as he lunged.

"It's too bad you don't have your little burned unicorn to help you," he taunted. "But that's what you get for taking her inside a dragon's cave."

There was no use even bothering to answer. But the spasm of rage at his mockery gave her a burst of extra strength.

Then, stepping backward, her foot sank into a small hole. She stumbled, and in the brief moment

. . . he stopped directly in front of her, and their two swords struck.

it took her to right herself, his sword battered into hers with such force that it was ripped from her hand. She stared in dismay as her weapon flipped end over end through the sunlight and came to rest in a small patch of weeds several metres away.

Left without any way to defend herself, she faced her uncle and waited. Her lungs struggled for air and her shoulder and arm throbbed. If she could stall him long enough, perhaps someone would come riding across the beach to save her. But somehow she didn't expect that to happen.

"Give me the flower," her uncle commanded, and pointed his sword at her throat.

Surely by now Connor and Perye had realized he wasn't on the boat with the trolls! They'd come looking for him, and for her . . .

"Your plan will never work," she said, stepping back from the weapon. "Grandmother will never make you king of North Bundelag, even if that means my mother sleeps forever. In all the time you spent with her as a boy, I'm surprised you didn't get to know her better. Grandmother can't be blackmailed."

A sudden gust of wind lifted his coattails and pulled the long, thin strands of his hair about his haggard face. He scowled and moved within an arm's length of her again, forcing her to take another step back.

"Give me the flower," he growled.

"You're the eldest son," she babbled on. "You're heir to the throne. If you mend your ways and try hard to win back Grandmother's trust, maybe she will — "

His forward lunge happened so quickly that it caught her off guard, though she'd been half expecting it. His grip felt as though it could break every bone in her wrist.

"Give it to me, now," he snarled, "or I will simply knock you down and take it."

This was it, then. It was over. She had run out of time. She swallowed the ache deep in her throat and raised her eyes to his.

"Let go of my wrist then," she whispered hoarsely. "It's in my pocket."

He dropped her wrist, though it continued to throb and her fingers to tingle. Slowly, with muscles that would hardly obey her will, she reached into her pocket and drew out the three small petals. They glittered in her palm like fragments of rainbow light torn from a rain-drenched sky. With a cry of victory, Raden reached out and scooped them from her hand.

Arica blinked, and then blinked again. The pieces of flower still trembled within her palm like tiny birds. Her uncle stared at her, then at his own empty hand. Rage exploded in his eyes. He grabbed for the petals again and again, but somehow they continued to elude him.

"Because they gave themselves to me," Arica whispered in awe.

The cry that burst from his lips sent a rush of such terror through her that she stumbled backward, desiring only to get as far away from him as she could. His face twisted above her and his sword whistled past her head. She fell to her knees with one arm raised to ward off the next blow.

"Stop right there," said a voice.

It was a calm and quiet voice, the kind of quiet that was clearer than a shout, the kind that compelled you to obey. A sudden relief washed through her, so intense it nearly made her faint. She knew that voice almost better than she knew her own.

"Grandmother," she said.

Neither Raden nor Grandmother paid her any attention. They just stood in awful silence with their gazes locked, while the air snapped and sizzled between them and grew hot with gathering power. The pressure of their anger mounted until Arica feared the outcome. Then just short of the breaking point, Raden turned away. She watched from her place on the sand as he whistled the stallion to his side, flung himself onto its back, and kicked it into a gallop.

A moment later Grandmother pulled Arica into

her arms, and she stayed there until long after her uncle had disappeared from sight.

"I'm so glad you're safe," was all the old woman said.

The next thing Arica knew, Connor, Perye and Drusa were scrambling across the beach toward them, all talking at once with three different versions of the same story. It was clear that they had successfully driven off the trolls, but just who had dealt the winning blow was an issue they couldn't seem to agree upon.

Arica couldn't help but grin, for she knew that deep down, not one of them really cared about who was the bravest or who had fought the best. They were just relieved that it was over and that everyone was all right.

"You're all heroes to me," she assured them. "Thank you. I couldn't have done it without you." Then she turned to Grandmother and took her by the arm.

"Let's go make my mother well," she said.

It didn't happen in the Fairy Village, though Arica was in a desperate hurry to see her mother awake and healthy again.

"It's better if she never learns about Bundelag," explained Grandmother as she, Arica, Connor and Nue sailed up the River of Songs with Mother sleeping in the boat. Grandmother had told them that with the wind in their favour and a bit of magic to push them along, this would be the easiest and quickest way to travel. Eventually they would leave the small sailboat behind and finish the journey on foot, bearing Arica's mother on a travois that Connor and Nue would pull.

Grandmother continued, "It would grieve her terribly to know that she is preventing your father from coming home, merely by being human. She doesn't need that kind of pain in her life."

All Arica could do was nod. "You know my mother well," she agreed.

At last they arrived at the entrance to Earth and, with Nue's help, carried Mother through the crack into Grandmother's house, and laid her gently on the bed. After Nue had gone, Grandmother and Arica brewed the magic tea and brought the cup into the bedroom. As it cooled, the three of them gazed at it in amazement. The tea was like the flowers. It sparkled with every colour in the rainbow and smelled like sweet honey and dewdrops and roses all mixed into one. When it was cool enough, Grandmother lifted Mother's head and Arica gently pressed the cup against her lips. As the magical liquid trickled into her mouth she swallowed once, then again and again. It was the first sign of life Arica had seen in her since she had fainted into Raden's arms those many days ago.

. . . Arica brewed the magic tea and brought the cup into the bedroom.

For a moment nothing happened. Then her mother's eyes opened and blinked in puzzlement as she gazed from Arica to Grandmother to Connor and back again.

"Arica . . . Mother . . ." she said, her voice hardly stronger than a whisper. "I had the strangest dream."

Then with a sigh her eyes fell closed once more — not in a sleep of death this time, but in a sleep of healing.

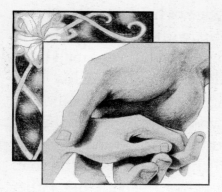

Epilogue

Arica's father knocked on her bedroom door. She knew it was her father because it was her father's kind of knock — hard and quick, and only two taps long. Mother's was more like a series of little patters, and Grandmother's — well, Arica couldn't remember the last time Grandmother had come knocking on her door. It must have happened once or twice in the past, for something in her childhood memories seemed to suggest it. But Grandmother no longer had time for tucking in children, not with a war to be won and a country to be saved from falling into ruin.

"Come in," she called.

Her father sat on the edge of her bed as he always did, and smiled down at her with fondness. Then, as always, he took her hand in his. Her own small hand all but disappeared inside it. She studied his hand thoughtfully. It was long-fingered and fine-boned, exactly the kind of hand you would expect to find on a king. She had always thought so, even before she found out how very nearly he had been exactly that.

"I'm not as thick-headed as I seem," her father announced. "Every once in a while, I do notice what's going on around me. I arrive home to find my wife ill and thin. My mother looks like she's aged five years in the past two weeks, and when I confront her about it, she just evades the question. All very unusual. But it is you, my dear princess, who make me wonder most of all."

"Me?" Arica squeaked, trying to sound as if she had no idea what he meant.

"Yes, you," he replied. "You've changed. You're more serious, more intense, a little sadder and much wiser. I can see it in your eyes. Do these changes have anything to do with a place called Bundelag?"

She froze in surprise. After a long stretch of rather strained silence, she managed to gather her wits enough to speak. "What do you remember about Bundelag?" she asked.

"Everything," he said, very quietly. "It's been coming back to me gradually for a while now, but during these past few weeks I've remembered almost everything."

Arica thought of what the fairy Tansley had told her back at the Fairy Village and nodded. "Like what?" she asked.

"I remember that my mother is a queen who married a commoner."

A commoner? Grandfather was a lot of things, but in her opinion common wasn't one of them. "Go on," she said.

"I remember that he never quite settled into the 'prince consort' role. I remember my elder brother, and the Fairy Village. And I remember the great variety of creatures that lived in that land." He paused, then added as he studied her face, "I remember the unicorns."

She had waited so long to have this conversation that now it was finally happening, she could hardly get her mind to accept it as real.

"Will you come with me next time?" she asked.

He shook his head, almost wearily. "I might visit there some day," he conceded. "But I'll never go back to live. How could I, without your mother?" He shrugged his shoulders helplessly. "Uncle Fred is in the same predicament. I suppose you know that he's a fairy, too?"

"Yes," she admitted.

His arms wrapped around her and pulled her close

against him. "I've done a lot of thinking about this," he said, "and I've concluded that whatever it is I'm supposed to do there, maybe — just maybe — you are meant to do it for me."

Arica tried to shake her head to protest such a great responsibility, but found that she couldn't with her face pressed so firmly against his shoulder. So she just remained there in comfortable silence and thought only of good and happy things, like Wish, who loved her, and her mother alive and nearly well in the next room. And then, some time later, when her father eased her gently down into the blankets, she was too warm and drowsy to argue. She was asleep before she even reached the pillow.

Vicki Blum lives in High River, Alberta,
where she enjoys going for long walks
and looking at the mountains.
As an elementary-school librarian,
she loves working with books and doing
workshops with young writers.
The Promise of the Unicorn is the fourth
adventure in her best-selling
unicorn fantasy series.

When Arica falls through a crack in her grandmother's kitchen floor, she finds herself in a strange world of fairies, trolls, elves and — best of all — unicorns. But the trolls and their evil master, Raden, take her prisoner, just as they have the unicorns. Fortunately, Arica discovers that she can hear the thoughts of the unicorns, in a way that no one else in this world seems able to do.

With the help of Wish, a playful young unicorn, Arica sets out to free the captives — and discover the true reason she was brought to this magical land.

Wish Upon a Unicorn
by Vicki Blum
ISBN 0-590-51519-5
$4.99

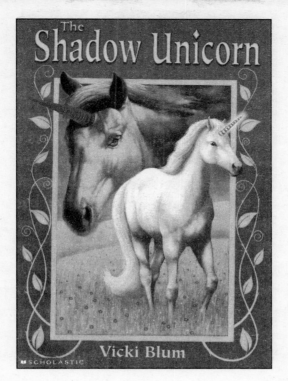

The Shadow Unicorn

Vicki Blum

SCHOLASTIC

Through a half-open window the wind moans, as if in pain. *Help us, True One,* it seems to say, as it whispers through the leaves.

So begins Arica's return journey to the magical land of unicorns, fairies and trolls. She arrives to find that the evil Raden is on the loose once again. With the help of a traitorous unicorn named Shadow, he has turned all the other unicorns to stone — all except Arica's friend, Wish.

Now it's up to Arica and Wish to stop them, and to bring the unicorns back to life.

The Shadow Unicorn
by Vicki Blum
ISBN 0-439-98706-7
$4.99

Arica has been summoned to North Bundelag and given a very important task: to cross over to South Bundelag, where cruel humans rule and unicorns dare not venture, and bring back the *Book of Fairies*. But this ancient treasure is in the hands of a greedy human merchant. And worse yet, the "horse" she's been given is actually the unicorn Shadow — her foe from an earlier battle.

Shadow says he is sorry for all he has done. But can Arica really trust him?

The Land Without Unicorns
by Vicki Blum
ISBN 0-439-98863-2
$4.99